Book Three
The Summer of Magic Quartet

Heart of the Hill

Andrea Spalding

D1501991

Orca Book Publishers

National Library of Canada Cataloguing in Publication Data

Spalding, Andrea
Heart of the hill / Andrea Spalding.

(The summer of magic quartet ; 3)
ISBN 1-55143-486-5

I. Title. II. Series: Spalding, Andrea Summer of magic quartet ; 3.

PS8587.P213H42 2005   jC813'.54   C2005-903270-7

First published in the United States, 2005
Library of Congress Control Number: 2005927693

Summary: Book Three of the Summer of Magic Quartet, in which Adam
must recover Myrddin's staff from the heart of Glastonbury Tor.

Orca Book Publishers gratefully acknowledges the support for its publishing
programs provided by the following agencies: the Government of Canada
through the Book Publishing Industry Development Program (BPIDP),
the Canada Council for the Arts, and the British Columbia Arts Council.

Cover image: Martin Springett

Orca Book Publishers
PO Box 5626, Station B
Victoria, BC Canada
V8R 6S4

Orca Book Publishers
PO Box 468
Custer, WA USA
98240-0468

www.orcabook.com
Printed and bound in Canada

09 08 07 06 05 • 6 5 4 3 2 1

For David,
who always believed it would happen.

Come by the hills, to the land
where legend remains;
Where stories of old stir the heart,
and may yet come again;
Where the past has been lost,
and the future is still to be won.
And the cares of tomorrow must wait
till this day is done.

Traditional folk song

NOTE: Myrddin is pronounced "merthin" and is the Celtic form of Merlin. "Traa dy liooar" is Manx, the Celtic language of the Isle of Man. It means "time enough" and is pronounced "trae de lure."

TABLE OF CONTENTS

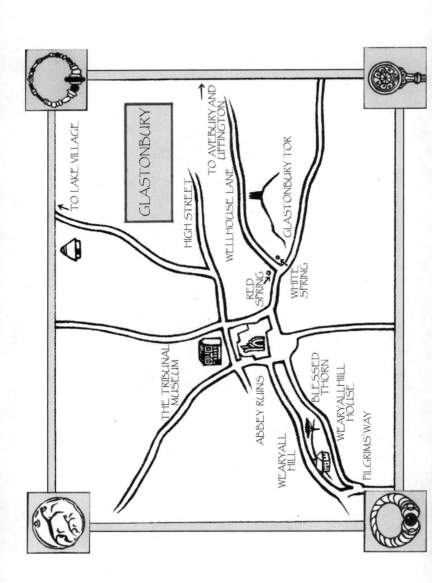

GLASTONBURY

TO LAKE VILLAGE

TO AVEBURY AND LIFFINGTON

HIGH STREET

WELLHOUSE LANE

GLASTONBURY TOR

RED SPRING

WHITE SPRING

THE TRIBUNAL MUSEUM

ABBEY RUINS

BLESSED THORN

WEARYALL HILL HOUSE

WEARYALL HILL

PILGRIMS' WAY

CHAPTER ONE

COME BY THE HILL

A midsummer moon rose over dark hills and flooded the sleeping valley with light—a brittle light, a white light, a light full of magic. The light slid into hidden places, and night prowling creatures retreated in confusion.

The moonlight washed like crystal water over the valley's fields. It flooded the small town that huddled around the base of the tower-topped hill that rose from the valley's heart. The moonlight concentrated its magic on the hill, known by the local people as the Tor.

Such clarity of light had rarely been seen in the heart of England. Only one set of eyes witnessed it now.

The watcher gazed down in awe as the Tor soaked up the magic.

The moon rose higher and higher, so bright and full that the watcher on the tower shielded her eyes.

Moonbeam by moonbeam the Tor drank in the magic, until its crystal heart beat strong, and the forgotten edges of the ancient labyrinth that climbed its slopes glowed.

Still the moonlight poured down. The Tor drank till it could drink no more. Three large, white, oval stones on its flanks shone with an inner radiance. Two stones marked the entrance to the forgotten spiral path. The third gleamed like an eye, high on the Tor's flank at the path's goal.

After centuries of slumber, the Spiral Labyrinth was awake.

From the tower top, the watcher lifted her arms to the moon and felt her own long-dormant powers course again through her veins. She quickly wove the moonlight into protective armor, for who knew what other beings the magic light had roused?

The moon reached its zenith, and its brittle light reflected and danced over the valley's rain-sodden fields. The Tor loomed like an island from the sea of light.

The watcher gasped, performed an ancient ritual and gave voice to the long forgotten prophecy.

> "When the Tor an island be,
> A child shall wind around the key
> And waken me."

She turned her face to the sky and laughed as clouds once again obscured the magical moon and raindrops fell upon her cheeks.

Her time had come.

<hr/>

Many miles distant, a child lay dreaming.

Adam knew he was dreaming, but he was scared. At first the dream had seemed only odd, but now he wanted desperately to wake. He could not. He was powerless to do anything but dream.

He'd fallen eagerly into bed, hoping his dreams would show him Myrddin, the magical being he'd promised to help. Instead, his dream had taken him to a strange place. He was standing beside a moonlit lake, staring across its water toward an island formed by a tower-topped hill.

Tendrils of magic flowed from the tower. They curled and tugged at Adam's dream self, trying to draw him across the water. He twisted and turned to avoid the magic. He didn't want to approach the island. It frightened him.

A voice from the tower spoke to him.

Come to the Tor. The words slipped through the dream and fixed themselves in his mind. *Come to Glastonbury Tor.*

Adam understood that was the name for the strange hill.

Reflected in the lake below, the Tor's steep sides were etched by a spiral path. The magic pulled at Adam's feet. He was supposed to walk the path.

Tread the Spiral Labyrinth. The whisper floated into his mind.

Adam's eyes traced the spiral path up toward the tower. He shivered. He was never going to climb up there. The power oozing from the place terrified him.

In his sleep, Adam burrowed under his duvet. In his dream, cold fear persisted.

Again, the black tower drew him. The archway that pierced the tower held Adam's eyes. He gazed through to the sky on the other side.

Come, child! Enter the Portal between worlds and you shall wield undreamed-of power, urged the whisper in Adam's head.

A helmeted knight strode through the archway and stared across the lake toward Adam.

The knight was a small distant figure, but in the clarity of the dream Adam could see every detail. He shrank back from piercing eyes and hung his head.

The knight placed the tip of his sword squarely on the ground in front of him and rested his hands on the hilt. The jewel-encrusted scabbard flashed and sparkled in the sunlight. Adam averted his eyes.

You cannot ignore me forever, for you are a Magic Child. My mind-probe has reached you and I can enter your dreams at will, said the voice. Adam heard the hint of a threat in its whisper. The pull of the magic grew stronger.

Adam fought against it, but the magic forced him to lift his eyes and look across the water at the knight.

The knight raised an arm and removed his helmet.

Adam gasped.

A tumble of golden hair fell around the armored shoulders. The knight was a beautiful young woman. She threw back her head and laughed.

Vivienne. The name slid into Adam's mind.

Adam fumed. He didn't like being tricked, and he didn't like beings invading his mind and making him do things. "Stop it, whoever you are. Leave my dreams alone!" he yelled.

Jewels flashed as Vivienne raised her sword in salute. *So! You do hear me.*

"Of course I hear you. You're whispering in my head!" Adam yelled across the lake. "Quit it."

"I have summoned you," answered Vivienne. This time her voice traveled clearly over the water. "Come."

Adam shuddered. *"No!* You can't make me!" He forced his feet to turn and run from the lake, away from the woman warrior, back through his dream and into reality.

"Adam...*Adam*...what's up?"

Adam woke to find his cousin Owen shaking his shoulder.

"Are you all right?" Owen's voice was anxious. "You were thrashing around and yelling."

Befuddled, Adam gazed around the moonlit bedroom. He wasn't in his Canadian bedroom...Where was he? Ah yes, he was staying with his cousins, in England. He struggled to make his mind work. "The lake," he muttered. "I was running from Vivienne and the lake."

"You're dreaming. You've had another nightmare, the third this week," said Owen. "Dream of something else. Something quieter."

Adam grinned groggily. "Sorry I woke you." He turned over and found a comfortable spot on the pillow. "I'll think of Myrddin. He will protect me." Adam conjured up the image of his favorite Wise One, the bearded man with the magical cloak. Keeping the image firmly in his mind, he drifted off to sleep.

Within the Portal below the dark tower on Glastonbury Tor, Vivienne sparkled with excitement. It had been well over a thousand years since her mind had connected with a human mind. Over two thousand years since she had been bound, against her will, as the Portal Keeper. Thousands of boring years, watching her power fade as humans forgot not only her, but Old Magic, and the ancient role of the Tor.

Vivienne cut a glittering swath through the darkness with her sword. "At last someone hears me. 'Tis only a child, but he is a Magic Child. Old Magic is stirring again!" She paused. "I wonder why the power is growing." She laughed and swung her sword again. "No matter. I have reached a human mind. The child will become more responsive with each probe." She dropped the tip of her sword to the ground and stood, feet apart, hands folded on the jeweled hilt, and sent her mind toward the boy once again.

The probe rushed forth, but Adam's sleep was guarded.

Vivienne shouted with frustration. She knew the image in the child's head. "The boy has met Myrddin. The Wise Ones have returned! That is why Old Magic stirs again." She pondered for a moment. Then she chuckled. "No matter. Old Magic is almost gone from Gaia. Myrddin is no more than a half-forgotten fairy tale. His fire burns low, and few believers follow the old ways. His staff is hidden, its power dormant. Without it, he is nothing." She laughed again. "My time has come. My new power makes me his equal! I will send him a sign. I will show Myrddin that in this new age, I am a force to be reckoned with."

Once more Vivienne concentrated. Her sword glittered with energy.

In response, the probe darted upward and swirled among the clouds above the child's house. The clouds thickened and became a storm. Torrential rains battered the small village of Uffington. As the wind strengthened, the probe surged back and forth under the cover of the darkness, leaving Vivienne's mark on the lawn. Then, its task completed, it darted back to the Tor.

The storm raged on.

Adam, Owen and Holly woke early. Only Chantel slept in. Adam banged on the bedroom door. "Wake up, Chantel! Everyone's eaten breakfast."

Chantel tugged on a sweater. She yawned. "I'm awake," she called. "Come in if you like."

Adam opened the door. "Seen the weather? It's gross. I don't think much of summer in England."

Chantel pulled the curtains back. Together she and Adam stared at the rain pouring from the thatched roof of the old farmhouse and thought about the endless golden days of a Canadian prairie summer.

Thunder rumbled.

Chantel shivered. "Ugh. I'm staying in today. It was a storm like this that made Snowflake throw me." She rubbed the cast on her broken leg.

Adam raised his eyebrows. "So? You wish it hadn't happened? That we'd never met the Wise Ones?"

Chantel gave a tiny chuckle. "Of course not. It's been amazing, hasn't it?" She wrinkled her nose. "But I wish the Wise Ones would hurry up and come back, like they said they would. Hasn't Myrddin visited your dreams yet? Equus talks to me in dreams."

Adam frowned. "No," he said shortly.

Chantel moved away, sensing one of her brother's snubs, but to her surprise he turned toward her.

"I am having spooky dreams, Chantel...nightmares. It's not Myrddin who's talking to me." Adam shrugged helplessly. "It's a warrior woman called Vivienne. She wants me to climb a hill somewhere, but I'm scared. What if she's one of the Dark Being's supporters, not the Wise Ones'?"

Before Chantel could answer, the bedroom door shook under another pounding.

"Hey, Chantel, you slept through a heck of a storm. The road to Uffington is flooded, and part of our paddock is underwater," bellowed her cousin Owen. "Can we come in?"

Adam opened the door.

"Want to go boating?" continued Owen. "There's a tin horse trough in the horse barn. I bet it will float."

Crack!

Chantel clapped her hands over her ears against the thunder. Her face blanched.

"It's okay, Chantel. Owen's being an idiot," soothed Holly, entering behind her brother.

Owen opened his mouth to protest, but Holly poked his back. "Don't be stupid, Owen. You know what happened last time Chantel was out in a storm."

Owen glanced guiltily at the cast on Chantel's leg. "Sorry! I forgot."

"It's okay," murmured Chantel. She moved clumsily from the window and sat on her bed. "My cast is coming off tomorrow. I'll be able to keep up with you soon." She gave a lopsided grin.

Lightning flashed and the almost instant thunder made her smile fade. She pulled the duvet around her head and shoulders.

"That was close!" Adam peered outside again. He could just make out patches of garden between rain gusts. It was wrecked. Tall blue delphinium spikes sprawled across the path instead of standing upright in the flower border. He looked more closely. The lawn seemed to be flattened in a circular pattern. "Er, guys... have you seen the lawn?" he said slowly.

Holly joined Adam at the window. She wiped the glass with her sleeve and peered out. "Good grief, look at the grass—we've got a crop circle." Holly rushed out of the room. The others heard her running down the stairs.

Adam and Owen followed.

Chantel sighed and limped along behind.

"What's a crop circle?" Adam asked as they pulled on rubber boots.

"Haven't you heard of them in Canada?" said Owen. "They're gigantic circular patterns found in grain fields. They were first discovered around here. They are really spectacular. Some people think they are made by aliens."

Light dawned on Adam's face. "I've seen a program about them on TV," he said. "On 'Ripley's Believe it or Not.' I didn't know they were from England. They're amazing." He took a deep breath. "So flying saucers land here. Wow!"

His cousins burst out laughing.

"Mom says it's the young farmers keeping busy," said Holly.

Adam looked puzzled. "You mean chasing flying saucers?"

"Nope, making the crop circles. It's field art—kind of like graffiti in a cornfield. Then tourists pay to photograph them," said Holly.

"Two locals were caught and prosecuted last year," added Owen. He paused and frowned. "But why would anyone bother to make one on our lawn?"

"The ones on TV weren't made by people," Adam said. "They were too big, and the designs were too complicated. It's not possible."

"Do you honestly think aliens make them?" Holly asked as she led the way into the garden.

Adam pointed to the lawn. "Something weird sure made that."

The grass was neatly flattened and swirled into a complicated circular pattern—a spiral that looped back and forth.

"Freaky," said Chantel. "Did one of you make it? As a joke?" She looked round the group, but everyone shook their heads.

"It's a spiral labyrinth," Adam said slowly.

Everyone stared at him.

"How do you know that?" demanded Holly.

Adam shrugged. "Dunno. I just do. I've had weird dreams where a voice in my head tells me to go to a hill and walk a spiral labyrinth...and...and...I just know that's the name for this pattern."

"Then it's Myrddin in your dreams," said Owen firmly. "That's how Ava contacted me. This must be a sign from him."

Adam shook his head. "It isn't. I haven't heard from Myrddin since you found Ava's circlet." He hunched his shoulders "This doesn't feel right. I bet the woman in my dreams made it. She's called Vivienne, and last night she whispered to me. She's trying to make me walk the 'Spiral Labyrinth.'" Adam shuddered. "I don't trust her. What if she's evil, like the dragon in our first adventure? What if she's from the Dark Being?"

Chantel moved closer to her brother. "We better be careful. The Wise Ones said a dark cloud was coming."

She looked up at the glowering sky. "Do you think this is it?"

The cousins stared at the clouds scurrying by, but they just looked like the normal aftermath of a storm.

Holly took charge. "If Adam thinks this is evil, let's get rid of it. Now, before the parents ask questions."

She ran to the garden shed, grabbed a rake and tossed a second to Owen.

From their place in the stars, the Wise Ones looked down at the small blue planet they called Gaia and humans called Earth.

"The storms grow fiercer, and the humans grow angrier and more warlike," said Equus, the great White Horse. He shifted restlessly, snorting and shaking his head. His mane and tail glinted with silver sparks. "The Dark Being nears, and the humans react to her influence."

Ava, the beautiful hawk woman, spread a wing and touched his back. "The children will prevail. They have retrieved your talisman and my circlet. Now that they are rested, they will help Myrddin regain his staff. Once we all have retrieved our tools from their hiding places, we can subdue the Dark Being despite her might and fury." She turned to Myrddin. "Go, retrieve your staff of power with young Adam. This task should be simple for the place of concealment is still honored by humans though most have forgotten why. Adam understands Earth Magic. He will walk the Labyrinth willingly and enter the Crystal Cave beneath the Tor."

"What will you do?" rumbled Myrddin. "Assemble our defenses?" He swished his cloak and its hidden colors danced like flames.

Equus sighed. "You are right, Myrddin. Though war is not our nature, the time has come for defense. Ava and I will travel to the Place Beyond Morning and ready it for the Lady's wakening and homecoming. We will use my talisman and Ava's circlet to restore the Silver Citadel and the great Gates of Sunrise so we can rebalance the approaching Dark with more Light."

"Light and Dark, Dark and Light," intoned Myrddin. "The balance will not be kept until we are linked again by the Lady's necklace."

Ava sighed. "Ah...the Lady! It has been so long since we felt her presence. Myrddin, take out the crystal. Let us look upon her once more."

Myrddin removed a small crystal ball from his pocket and set it spinning in the air.

Ava stretched out her wings and she, Equus and Myrddin formed a circle with the spinning crystal in the center.

"A talisman to hone the mind,
A circlet old to hold and bind,

A staff to smite with hidden might,
Beads to link, and hold the light," they chanted.

The flashes of light shimmered, formed and reformed as images from the past appeared in the crystal.

Equus, Myrddin and Ava saw themselves, once again, inside the Silver Citadel.

Tears brightened Ava's eyes. "I remember this moment. Look at the Lady, so calm, so wise and so beautiful. Myrddin, may we hear as well as see?"

Myrddin sprinkled stardust over the spinning globe.

Their ears rang with the sound of the Dark Being's furious final onslaught on the Place Beyond Morning.

They stared as the tiny figures within the crystal surrendered the tools of power.

"The Lady fingers her necklace," murmured Ava. "She felt our pain."

They listened intently to the Lady's voice.

"Without these tools of power, the Dark Being will find victory brings nothing."

"Destroy these, and we are nothing," *replied the voice of Equus.*

"The Lady's smile is heartbreaking," said Ava.

"Hush!" reproved Myrddin. The Wise Ones bent their heads again toward the crystal to catch the reply.

"Conceal, not destroy!" *came the Lady's voice.* "In a galaxy known as the Milky Way spins an almost unnoticed misty blue planet. On it are many places of great beauty, among them an island known as Angel Land named after the fair-haired race that inhabits it. Those people will honor your tools and keep them safe. The talisman, staff and circlet will be hidden in the center of Angel Land."

Myrddin shifted as he heard his own voice interrupt. "And the necklace, Lady?"

"That I must guard. A smaller isle lies off the coast of Angel Land. It is home of a mage called Manannin, who keeps his isle hidden within a cloak of mist. I will hide there. Go swiftly and safely on the wings of dawn my friends. Conceal your magic tools in Angel Land, trust in the humans and leap for the stars to watch over them. The necklace and I must sleep behind Manannin's Cloak. As long as the beads and I stay linked, so shall the magic link us all."

The scene faded.

Myrddin reached out a hand. One finger gently stopped the spinning crystal. He replaced it in his pocket.

Equus sighed. "Thank you, Myrddin. The Lady's courage gives me hope and strength."

Ava looked worried. "But what has happened to her? The mist of Manannin must be thick and all enclosing or she would be awake to guide us. Even in sleep, the necklace should warn of the Dark Being's approach."

Equus stirred uneasily.

16

Myrddin's brows met. "The Lady answers to no one. We must trust and believe. *Traa dy liooar*, remember? Time enough...*Traa dy liooar*."

"But IS there time enough?" Equus gave voice to the fear deep in their hearts.

Ava pulled herself up and spread her wings. Her light blazed. "NOW is the time. We will ready the Place Beyond Morning and wake her."

"Then farewell friends," said Myrddin gruffly. "Travel safely among sunbeams, for the Dark Being abhors the light. I will work alone on Gaia with the Magic Children." He flung back his head and swung his cloak. "Adam, are you ready? I come!" he roared. His hair and beard blazed with inner fire.

"Wait" Ava laid a wing tip on his arm. "Equus and I cannot leave Chantel and Owen without explanation."

Equus agreed. "They too can help. They must persuade other humans to keep the light."

Myrddin snorted. "Not easy."

"May light flicker always in human hearts." The blessing voiced by Ava drifted through the heavens as the three Wise Ones wove among sunbeams toward Gaia.

CHAPTER TWO

The Cares of Tomorrow

The children's entire day was stormy.

The thunderstorm showed no sign of abating, and Owen sulked when his father prevented him from boating on the floodwaters.

Holly and Chantel organized a game of Scrabble, but the four cousins couldn't agree.

"That's not fair. Those dumb two-letter things aren't real words. We never use them in Canada," protested Adam.

"If everything is so great in Canada, why don't you go back?" retorted Owen.

"I will as soon as my idiot parents stop arguing and send for us," Adam shouted. He left the table, knocking the board. The game pieces scattered.

Everyone began yelling.

"Can we bake cookies?" Chantel asked a little later.

Even Adam brightened at that suggestion.

Aunt Lynne shooed them out of the kitchen.

"But, Mum...Chantel and Adam know how to make chocolate chip cookies," said Owen.

"Not today," said Lynne as she rolled out pastry. "I've promised gooseberry pies for the museum's fundraising dinner tonight. There's plenty of biscuits in the tin if you want a snack."

"Not with chocolate," muttered Owen.

His mother rolled her eyes.

The phone rang. Everyone jumped.

Lynne held up her floury hands. "Could one of you catch that? It's probably the hospital confirming Chantel's appointment."

Owen and Adam dived for the phone. Their heads met with a clunk. They rubbed foreheads and glared at each other.

Holly giggled and picked up the receiver. "White Horse Farm, Holly speaking." Her face grew wary. "Oh, hello." She turned uneasily to her mother, her hand over the mouthpiece. "It's for Adam and Chantel," she hissed. "It's Aunt Celia, but she's crying."

Adam pushed past Owen.

Lynne swiftly wiped her hands on her apron and took the receiver. She motioned Adam and Chantel to wait.

"Goodness, Celia, what time is it in Canada? It's only mid-morning here...three AM! Why can't you sleep?"

She listened for a moment, a frown gathering between her eyes. "Yes, Chantel and Adam are here."

Chantel and Adam stared at their aunt. There was an odd tone in her voice.

Lynne turned away from them and dropped her voice. "Do you think that's wise, Celia? Shouldn't you get some rest and speak to them later...No...Of course I'm not keeping your children from you..."

Chantel slipped her hand into Adam's. They both squeezed hard, their faces anxious as they listened to the tinny sound of their mother's voice leaking from the receiver. Was she upset, or angry, or both?

"If you hold the line, Celia, I'll let them take this in the office, so they can have some privacy." Lynne handed the mobile phone to Adam and motioned them into the small farm office off the kitchen. She pulled out the desk chair for Chantel and passed her the office phone. "I'll be outside if you need me," she whispered and closed the door.

Chantel picked up the receiver. "Hi, Mom." Her voice trembled.

"At last. Is Adam there too?"

"I'm here."

"Are you both okay?"

"We're fine, but you're not, are you?" Adam's voice was tight and hard. "You and Dad have been fighting again, haven't you?"

"Don't, Adam," whispered Chantel. The knuckles of her hands were white as they clutched the receiver.

"How did you guess?" There was a muffled sound as though their mother was swallowing a sob. "Adam... Chantel...I'm sorry...there is no easy way about this, so I'm just going to say it. You're right...your father...he's left. That is...we both still love you, but we don't love each other anymore. We're getting a divorce."

"Oh, nice," said Adam. "Dad loves us so much he's taken off, and you're phoning to say you're getting a divorce. So, what about me and Chantel?"

"That's all you can say? You're only worried about you?" shrieked his mother.

"What do you want us to say—yip-dee-doo? You think we didn't guess about the divorce?" said Adam. "You think we don't know why you packed us off to England?"

"We wanted to make it easier for you," said his mother. "We wanted to save you from the arguments."

"Yeah, right," said Adam. "You're thinking about us so much that not only are you splitting but—"

Chantel's soft voice interrupted them. "Where's Daddy gone?"

"He didn't say, honey. He just left."

"Oh." Tears spilled down Chantel's cheeks.

"I'm sorry, honey. I'm really sorry, but it doesn't mean that we don't love you." There was a sob and her mother's voice choked up. "I...I know your father will call you."

"Who cares?" stormed Adam. "We don't. You did nothing but yell at us when we were home, then you shipped us off to another country, so why should we care? Neither of you care about us, and we don't care about you." He hurled the mobile phone across the room and stormed out of the office, slamming the door.

"Adam, Adam."

"There's only me," said Chantel. Her voice was almost a whisper.

"I'm so sorry, Chantel. I didn't mean to hurt you. I'll call again, honey." The line hummed in Chantel's ear as her mother's voice broke and she rang off.

As emotional storms raged through the Maxwell household, the Dark Being stormed across the Milky Way and rent her fury on yet another small star. Nothing was hidden there.

"The Wise Ones have concealed the tools of power well," she raged, "I WILL find them."

She knew she was finally in the right galaxy for she could sense their presence—a tingling and a brightness in the air. She pulled the darkness closer, to shield her and her supporters from the hated light, but suddenly she felt remnants of the Wise Ones' thoughts winging through the air...a feeling of hope and purpose. It was as though the Wise Ones were near, were aware of her movements and were outwitting her. How could that be?

The Dark Being sent a roar of anger boiling across the universe. "I hear you, Wise Ones...You shall not escape me this time." She directed her cohorts to the other stars and planets around her. "Go! Seek them!"

Her second-in-command, Zorianna, sped toward Gaia.

✦✦✦✦

Holly and Owen watched as Adam slammed the office door and pushed past them. He headed up the stairs, his face so white the freckles stood out in blotches.

"Adam?" Owen called.

Adam kept on going.

Owen's mother put her hand on Owen's shoulder. "Let him be. He needs time alone. You can comfort him later on."

Owen leaned against his mother, and she gave him a quick hug, leaving traces of flour on his cheek.

"What about Chantel?" asked Holly.

"We'll give her a minute. She may still be on the phone with her mother," said Lynne.

Holly crept over to the door and listened.

"Holly!" Lynne protested.

"No one's talking, Mum, but Chantel's crying."

Lynne looked from her daughter to the closed door

and sighed. She walked over, knocked lightly and opened the door.

Chantel huddled in the office chair, her face hidden in her hands, her body shaking with sobs.

"Oh, you poor little thing." Lynne swept Chantel into her arms.

Holly closed the door gently.

Owen perched on the kitchen windowsill, his heels tapping the radiator on the wall. "So they've decided then. Aunt Celia and Uncle Brent are divorcing?"

Holly nodded. "It looks like it."

"What about Adam and Chantel?"

Holly shrugged.

* * *

Adam crouched on the bottom bunk bed and pounded his pillow again and again. "I hate them, I hate them, I hate them." He collapsed on the mattress and pulled the duvet over his body so not even his head was exposed. He was as cold as ice—frozen with fear. What was going to happen to him and Chantel?

Adam...Adam...ADAM. The voice in his head grew louder and more insistent.

Adam ignored it.

ADAM! This time the voice roared though his whole being, making his body tingle.

GO AWAY! Adam roared back in his mind.

The tingling grew stronger. *Adam...It is I...Myrddin. Don't you get it? I don't care*. Adam pulled the duvet even more tightly around his head. *Go away! I don't want to mindspeak.*

A gentle warmth washed over his body, and he felt the presence not only of Myrddin, but the fleeting touch of Ava's wing on his forehead and the soft breath of a horse by his ear. Despite his anger and fear, the warmth relaxed him. *Wise Ones, please go away. I can't help you now. Bad things are happening.*

He felt another touch of Ava's wings. *We understand, Adam. We feel your pain. But you are not the only human in despair. Many bad things are happening on Gaia. The Dark Being is close, and darkness stirs and thickens.*

Adam stirred. *You mean if the Dark Being goes away everything will be all right?* There was a pause. He slumped, sensing the answer before the Wise Ones spoke. *I know...You can't fix Mom and Dad. You can't make them stop fighting. No one can.*

You are correct, Adam. Myrddin sighed. *We cannot interfere between humans. We offer only the comfort of Light. We work with Old Magic and with those who willingly help, like you and the other Magic Children. We are with you, Adam. Use our strength. Our presence is around you. Light will ease your heartpain.*

The sense of comfort and warmth helped melt the ice in his body. Adam buried his face in his pillow and cried hot tears. The tears drained him, but somehow their falling eased his pain. The Wise Ones stayed with him, soothing him, and when at last he fell into exhausted sleep, Myrddin was waiting in his dream.

Myrddin's cloak enfolded Adam's dreamself and swept him into the sky. Adam welcomed the distraction. Unlike his parents, Myrddin needed him, and Adam liked that. He watched the small village of Uffington fall away below and with it all his problems. First a feeling of great speed and a rushing of wind, then he and Myrddin touched down on an unfamiliar hilltop.

Adam looked across a valley toward a small city bathed in sunlight. It huddled around the base of a tower-topped hill.

"Hey, that's Glastonbury Tor," said Adam. "B...but where did the city come from?" He stared down at the farmlands in the valley, flat fields crisscrossed with roads, ditches and dikes. "What happened to the lake?"

Myrddin's eyebrows raised. "You have traveled this way before?"

"Yes...I mean no...I mean...I had a nightmare and saw the Tor, only it was in the middle of a lake...and a warrior woman spoke to me from the tower."

"Vivienne!" said Myrddin in disgust. "Huh." He struck the ground with his walking stick.

"Yes, that's her name. Who is she? Is she bad news?" asked Adam.

Myrddin gave a bark of laughter. "Bad news? I suppose she is. Centuries ago she was my apprentice—until the lust for power overcame her, and she was imprisoned in the Tor." He pointed with his stick to the valley. "Your dream showed the Tor's past, when a marshy lake filled the valley. People lived on small islands, and the Tor, the biggest island, was named Avalon."

"Avalon!" said Adam eagerly. "As in King Arthur and the Isle of Avalon?"

Myrddin nodded slowly. "Yes, Glastonbury Tor is the Avalon of old. But King Arthur is different. Arthur was first Arto, a Magic Child like you. But memories of other Magic Children were woven into his story, so the tales of King Arthur are not about one person, but several."

Adam's face fell. "King Arthur wasn't real...what a crock!"

Myrddin gave a deep chuckle. "Arto was real, and a feisty young Celt he was. But the stories came later. They grew in the way that stories do." He laughed again and stretched his arms to the sky. "Even my role with Arto was misunderstood."

"Your role, Myrddin? You were with Arthur...I mean Arto?" gabbled Adam. "Hey, I get it! You're Merlin, aren't you? You're King Arthur's magician!"

Myrddin drew himself up. "I am the Myrddin," he rumbled. "I am no one's magician. I am the Myrddin, a Wise One, a keeper of Old Magic." His eyes flashed.

"Hey, okay...Okay...I'm sorry," stuttered Adam. "I didn't mean to insult you."

Myrddin softened. "Yes, I am the Myrddin, the one that humans called Merlin. But like the tales of Arthur, the stories of Merlin were woven by people to make sense of powers they didn't comprehend. The truth remains simple. I am a Wise One, and the Tor is the Portal to many worlds."

"That's what Vivienne said." Adam stared at the Tor.

"Within the Portal are many doors. Through them the past, present and future of many universes can be reached. Vivienne keeps watch. Beings who intend harm to Gaia are directed elsewhere."

"Then why are you worried about the Dark Being?" asked Adam.

"The Dark Being is the exception," said Myrddin heavily. "Like the Wise Ones, she does not need the Portal."

"Oh." Adam shrank into himself.

"Sometimes Vivienne becomes angry and misdirects Portal users." Myrddin sighed. "Sadly, she is often angry, for her job of Portal Keeper is a punishment."

"You punished her?" asked Adam.

Myrddin shook his head. "Not I. She didn't listen. Instead of honoring Old Magic, she thought she was strong enough to make it do her bidding. At that time I, the Myrddin, was Gaia's Portal Keeper and Vivienne was my assistant. I came and went as the need arose. Vivienne was jealous of my power. My staff lay in the Lady's sanctuary, the Crystal Cave, protected by the rituals of Avalon. But temptation overcame Vivienne. She learned enough Old Magic to enter the Crystal Cave, seize my staff and try to wield it. I regained control, but not before the magic Vivienne had conjured wrapped around and bound her forever as Portal Keeper. The Lady's high priestess used Earth Magic to conceal my staff again. The Crystal Cave was sealed and Avalon abandoned in the hope that all would forget what power sleeps in the heart of the hill."

"Wow! And Vivienne is Portal Keeper for ever?"

"Yes, unless..." Myrddin looked searchingly at Adam. "Unless someone breaks the spell by offering to take her place."

Adam shuddered. "No way! Vivienne gives me the creeps. I hate her whispering." He clapped his hands over his ears. "I wouldn't listen. I thought about you instead. But then I felt her presence again this morning."

Myrddin looked troubled. "When, Adam?"

"When a spiral labyrinth appeared on our lawn."

Myrddin stamped his stick on the ground again. "How dare she!" He glowered at the Tor. "Vivienne's power is growing as the Dark Being approaches. Be on your guard."

"No problem," said Adam. "I'm not going near her."

"Unfortunately it's not that simple," rumbled Myrddin.

Adam shrugged. "Look, just tell me how to get your staff, okay?"

Myrddin pointed toward the Tor. "You must tread the Spiral Labyrinth, enter the Portal and ask Vivienne to reveal the entrance to the Crystal Cave."

Adam's jaw dropped. "But...but...you told me to keep away from her."

"I said be on your guard; you cannot avoid her. Vivienne may distract you, offer you choices. Keep your destination clearly in mind so she cannot divert you. You can do this Adam. You have experienced dragon talk. You know how to ignore a silver tongue with promises of power."

Adam thought back to the first adventure and hung his head. "I failed," he muttered. "I believed the dragon."

"No," said Myrddin. "You did not fail. In the end you resisted the temptations the dragon offered. You encouraged Holly to sacrifice the talisman. That was not failure. You showed great strength."

Myrddin squeezed Adam's shoulder.

Adam trembled. "Myrddin, I'm scared."

Myrddin's face was sad. He said nothing.

Adam's voice shook. "I'll mess up again. Mom says I always mess up. Please...can't you do it?"

"The door and the treasure you seek are protected by Earth Magic," murmured Myrddin. "Earth, air, fire and water. Only humans can weave them together to lock and unlock Earth Magic at will."

Adam shuffled his feet. His stomach churned.

The wind freshened, and the sky grew dark. The ground trembled, and Adam and Myrddin staggered and grabbed at each other.

"What's happening?" cried Adam. "Was...was it an earthquake?"

Myrddin hushed Adam and knelt, placing his ear to the ground. "A quake indeed, but not of the earth, of Old Magic," he said finally, levering himself upright again. "An emissary from the Dark Being has found Gaia. She is challenging Vivienne and attempting a forced entry through the portal! Come...she must not sense us."

He threw his cloak over Adam, and they were gone.

CHAPTER THREE

Wait Till This Day is Done

Adam awoke with a sense of urgency.

He lay on his back and considered his dream, his mind racing.

He was relieved Myrddin had contacted him but fearful of facing the Spiral Labyrinth and Vivienne. What if he failed? What would happen to him? What was the worst Vivienne could do—make him Portal Keeper? Despite himself a wry grin lifted the corners of Adam's mouth. So what? Who cared? Not his parents! Considering the mess his life was in, being keeper of a magic portal almost sounded like fun. He could do magic and meet interesting beings from other worlds, plus he'd know what was happening to him for the next few hundred years. Adam laughed out loud. Yup, his dad had taken off, so why not him? If he disappeared to be Portal Keeper it would teach his folks a lesson! What the heck, he'd risk it. He had nothing to lose! Besides, unlike his parents, Myrddin needed him.

With new resolve and a sense of purpose Adam ran down the stairs into the kitchen, startling Holly who was reading in the big rocking chair by the window.

"Whoa...What's up?" she asked.

"We need to talk. Where are Owen and Chantel?" said Adam.

Holly shrugged. "I dunno where Owen went, but Chantel's in the bedroom with Mum." She lifted an eyebrow. "Are you okay? Did you sleep?"

Adam nodded. "Yes, yes. But I need everyone. We've gotta talk."

"I'm here, talk away. Is it about your parents?"

Adam shook his head. "They're the least of my worries. Myrddin just visited me." He glanced around to check that no adults were within earshot. "We've gotta do something quick. It's about the Dark Being. She's sent someone here," he hissed.

Holly's eyes widened. She looked around the room.

"Not here in the kitchen, idiot," said Adam. "To Gaia. I...I mean Earth. Myrddin said an emissary's come, and if she gets Myrddin's staff the Wise Ones are toast. We've got to get it first." Adam held up his hands. "I need help, Holly. It's terrifying. I've got to go to a place called Glastonbury Tor, face that woman from my nightmare and rescue the staff—quick! I don't even know where Glastonbury is!"

"It's a couple of hours southwest of here, in Somerset," said Holly promptly. "We've never been, but our neighbor Mr. Smythe gave a talk about Glastonbury at the Uffington Museum. It was really interesting." Holly became more excited. "There's a ruined abbey where King Arthur and Queen Guinevere are buried, and a big hill called the Tor. The Tor is where Merlin's imprisoned. He's supposed to be asleep in a Crystal Cave at its heart."

"Those stories aren't true," said Adam.

"Says who?" said Holly.

"Says Myrddin," said Adam. "But that's where his staff is...in the Crystal Cave. And you'll never guess who Myrddin really is!"

Holly gave a little gasp. "Of course...He's Merlin, isn't he? Fan-bloody-tastic!"

Lynne stopped rubbing Chantel's back and eased herself off the bed. She looked down sadly at her niece.

Chantel had fallen into an exhausted sleep following the emotional storm triggered by her mother's phone call.

"Life is just not fair, child," Lynne whispered. "You

didn't deserve this." She smoothed the bedcover and tiptoed out.

Can you hear me, child?

Chantel stirred in her sleep.

Chantel, I have news. Gentle mindspeak from Equus slid into her dream.

Despite her sorrow, Chantel's lips curved into a smile as she smelled the musky scent of the Great White Horse King and felt strands from his silky mane brush her cheek.

Hello, Horse. I've missed you. Can we go riding? I need some magic. In her dream, she twisted her hand into his mane and swung herself up on his back. *Please fix things.* Chantel leaned forward and hugged his neck. *Mom and Dad are so angry they are divorcing. They need fixing. Please, White Horse. Please.*

A feeling of comfort tinged with regret, swept over her.

I understand, Chantel. Adam told us. But you know we cannot interfere between humans.

Chantel sighed and stilled her cheek against the neck of the horse. Tears oozed between her lashes.

Peace, child. Believe in the light. Equus surrounded Chantel with warmth and light as he galloped through the stars. *"Comfort Chantel,"* he called to the night winds.

The night winds blew musically through Chantel's hair, tickling her ears, and despite her unhappiness, she gave a crooked smile and sat up.

Can you talk with me now, little one?

Guess so. What's up, Horse? Is Myrddin going to ask Adam for help?

He is, for help is sorely needed. An emissary from the Dark Being has entered your galaxy. Adam's task will be difficult. He and Myrddin need assistance from you all.

We'll help. You know that, Horse. Besides, you and Ava will be with us...won't you?"

There was a long pause.

Won't you? Chantel pulled on the horse king's mane. *You will...won't you?*

I fear not. Ava and I must return to the Place Beyond Morning. With the power from our talisman and circlet we can repair much of the devastation caused by the Dark Being and ready the Silver Citadel for the waking of the Lady.

The Lady? Chantel said.

The Lady, repeated Equus, his mindspeak full of love and respect. *The fourth and greatest of the Wise Ones. We must wake her so the power of her necklace will be rekindled.* He laughed. *You think I am magical? The Lady holds the magic of all worlds linked around her neck.* His mindspeak grew more serious. *Do you understand why I must leave you, child?*

Chantel's hand convulsed. She clutched Equus's mane even tighter. *Don't go. Don't leave me,* she cried. A tear ran down her cheek. *Everyone's leaving me. You mustn't go too!*

Be strong, Chantel. If all goes as planned, Ava and I will swiftly return. Nourish the light in your heart. Help Adam by sharing it with others, and it will grow. Come...I will show you.

With great strides that spanned the heavens, Equus bore Chantel beyond the Milky Way and across galaxies, galloping through clouds of stardust and along beams of sunlight from alien suns.

Despite her sadness, Chantel felt her heart lift as the music of the universe sang in her ears. She started to hum along.

That's it, child. Sing, urged Equus. *Sing with me.*

Chantel chuckled. *Horses can't sing.*

To her surprise Equus threw back his head, and a strangely beautiful song poured forth. The deep notes echoed and thrilled as they mixed with the wordless song around her. The joyous sound touched her heart so intensely she joined in.

Chantel's voice was true and sweet, not as high as the notes flowing around her, nor as low as Equus's voice; she sang the middle notes of a magical trio.

As she sang, her sadness lifted.

Your gift reflects your name, for Chantel means singer, said Equus, as their song died away. *Always remember this moment. Use your voice on Gaia to strengthen the light. When darkness lies heavy, songs bring comfort. Your voice is your tool. Use it.*

Chantel flushed with embarrassment and pride.

I didn't know I could sing, and now I have a tool. Wow!

Keep this moment always in your heart, counseled Equus. *When I am gone, remember your tool.*

I will, Chantel promised. She rode back through the stars and slipped off Equus's back into a deep healing sleep.

Owen spent the afternoon on his own. He lay on a pile of hay in the stable loft listening to the rain drumming on the roof and the ponies' feet shifting occasionally in the stalls below. He ate a handful of grapes one by one and passed the time spitting the seeds at a knot in the beam above him. He'd scored a bull's-eye twice in succession.

Thoughts buzzed around in his head: frustration at not being allowed to sail on the floodwaters, sympathy for Adam and Chantel, dislike for their parents and a rush of love for his own. Thank goodness they weren't going to divorce. He stirred uneasily. What would happen to Adam and Chantel? Would they come to live at White Horse Farm forever? "Oh, no. Not forever!" he groaned and sat up, coughing frantically as he inhaled a seed.

A scratching sound interrupted him. The ponies stilled and cocked their ears. Owen did the same.

The scratching came again.

Owen crawled over to the shuttered window at the far end of the loft. The sound came from the other side. He eased the bolts free, cracked opened the shutter and peered through.

A hawk was perched on the ledge.

"*Ava!*" Owen flung open the shutter and thrust out his arm. The hawk stepped onto his wrist, and he drew her inside.

Shhhh, no need to shout. Ava's reproof filled his head. *Mindspeak's easier and no one overhears.*

Owen grinned and held his arm against a hay bale.

Ava stepped off and smoothed her ruffled feathers with her beak. Her hawk eyes looked piercingly at Owen. *Greetings, Magic Child. You are none the worse for your experiences in my sanctuary?*

Owen shook his head. *No...though I was really scared when I thought you were dead.* He looked at her with loving eyes. *I was so relieved when you came to life again.*

You showed great courage and quick wit, Owen. You are indeed a young warrior. You lived up to the old meaning of your name.

Young warrior...that's what my name means? No one ever told me that. Owen looked pleased.

Owen, you must use your courage and quick wit to help Adam and Myrddin. You must all work together as a team, for the Dark Being is now aware of Gaia and has sent an emissary here. This means Adam's task will be dangerous.

Equus and I must leave you, for the Place Beyond Morning needs repair. We will use the renewed power of the talisman and circlet to rebuild the Silver Citadel and the Great Gates of Sunrise. Once they stand tall they will act as defenses. The Dark Being will find it harder to put out the light.

Owen caressed Ava's feathers. *I'll miss you.*

The hawk bowed her head, and Owen caught a glimpse of something glinting among her feathers.

"Oh!" Owen gasped, forgetting to mindspeak. "You're wearing your circlet!"

It is a permanent part of me, thanks to you and the other Magic Children. Ava spread her wings and grew, shape changing. For an instant Owen saw her towering above him, a shimmering, strangely beautiful hawk-woman, whose brow was crowned by a glowing twist of silver bands holding a white moonstone in the center.

A dark cloud passed the window and cut off the sun. The image faded away, and Ava shrank back to a small hawk once more. *I must go and rebuild. You will not hear from me until I return,* she continued. *Promise you will give Myrddin and Adam your aid.*

I'll help them, promised Owen. *So will Holly and Chantel.*

Ava's eyes bore deep into his heart. *Joining forces may not be easy. The Dark Being and her followers will sow discord and dissent. Alliances may be uneasy.*

With this remark the hawk spread her wings and soared from the hay bale, through the open shutters and toward the clouds. *Farewell, Owen. May light be always in your heart.*

Owen hung out of the window. "Good luck, Ava," he called and watched until she vanished.

⁂

"You mean *all* of you have been visited by a Wise One?" said Holly crossly. "What about me? Don't I count?"

Adam and Owen shifted on their seats and dropped their eyes.

"It...it's not that." Owen spread his hands wide. "It's just...well...There are only three Wise Ones," he finished with a rush.

Holly gave a snort of frustration.

"There's the Lady." Chantel's quiet voice caught everyone's attention.

Chantel flushed but held her ground. "You keep forgetting: there are four Wise Ones, the Lady's sleeping. She'll wake up soon. That's why Equus and Ava are going to the Place Beyond Morning. To get it ready for her."

"Right, Holly. You'll help the Lady," said Owen, relieved. "So let's get on with helping Adam. How are we going to get to Glastonbury?"

"Holly thought Mr. Smythe might know. He visits Glastonbury," said Adam. "He was pretty cool in the first adventure. He believed us about the magic, even though it never happened to him."

"Good idea, sis." Owen punched Holly's arm. "Come on, let's see if he's in." Grabbing his raincoat from the front hall, he yelled up the stairs to the office, "We're going round to visit Mr. Smythe, Mum...Okay?"

"Don't be late for tea," his mother replied.

"And don't call me 'sis,'" muttered Holly as she followed. The droop of her shoulders mirrored her disappointment and frustration.

Heads down against the driving rain, Adam and Owen ran up the flag pathway alongside the Big House. They passed the imposing entrance, heading instead for the small green back door. Adam arrived first. He rat-tatted on the lion's head knocker, grinned at Owen and jiggled impatiently.

Chantel limped behind as fast as she could, but Holly lagged even farther.

Holly felt moody and out of sorts. As the eldest she wasn't used to being overlooked. She kicked a pebble off the path and watched as it bounced over the grass sending up fine sprays of water. She tried giving herself a mental shake. This summer was incredible. They'd had two unbelievable adventures, and now they were beginning a third. But she was so fed up with being the eldest, being sensible and patient and helpful to the others. When would it be her turn to be important and help this invisible Lady? Holly stopped as a curl of anticipation stirred inside her. What would the Lady be like? Equus was the great White Horse King and Ava an amazing half-woman, half-hawk shape changer. Myrddin seemed the most human, though his red hair and beard and black cape of hidden colors made him almost spectacular. A tiny smile lifted the corners of Holly's mouth. The Lady would be beautiful. She could feel it in her bones. The Lady would be as beautiful as the raindrop diamonds sparkling on the grass. Feeling hopeful, Holly ran to catch up with the others.

"Welcome, welcome! What a good idea, a visit with friends will help unseasonable weather pass unnoticed." Mr. Smythe opened the door and waved them inside. He flattened his tall wiry frame against the wall so they could enter the cramped passageway and hang their dripping coats.

Adam was first into the familiar kitchen. He stepped onto the stone floor and took a deep breath—ah, the smell of old books! He gazed around the cluttered room with satisfaction. His mother never let him collect junk, and his few books were kept neatly on a shelf in alphabetical order. He gave a little shudder—who knew what would happen to them now.

Mr. Smythe's kitchen wasn't just where he cooked; it was where he lived. Books were piled on chairs, on the table and on the floor, creating a maze to edge through. Perched haphazardly among them were interesting archeological objects.

A plastic bowl full of sand supporting a glued pottery urn currently held pride of place on the large wooden table. Pieces of bone and geological samples were scattered along the edge of the kitchen dresser, jostling for space among the plates and cups. Cracked jugs and bits of metal from ancient bridles hung from hooks in the ceiling. The walls were covered with photos and maps, old maps, new maps and two giant aerial photos of the White Horse and the Red Horse that had started their adventures. Everywhere Adam looked there was something fascinating. This room was his idea of heaven.

Mr. Smythe gathered a scatter of papers together and tucked them between the pages of a reference book, clearing a space at the end of the table. Each child removed a pile of books from the nearest chair and placed them on the floor. Eventually everyone had a seat. They beamed at each other.

"To what do I owe the pleasure of your company?" asked Mr. Smythe, rubbing his hands together and stretching his fingers. "Are you in the middle of another interesting adventure?"

Owen did not beat about the bush. "We don't know yet, Sir," he said briskly. "We might be. We need to go to Glastonbury."

"Ahh." Mr. Smythe's eyes twinkled. "Glastonbury is it? Don't tell me...you are going to look for King Arthur's Holy Grail."

The kids shook their heads.

"Excalibur?"

They shook their heads even more vigorously.

Mr. Smythe sat back and waited.

Adam leaned forward over the table. "The truth is...well, we kind of don't really know yet what we have to do...But, but...have you ever heard of...the Spiral Labyrinth?"

Mr. Smythe thought for a minute, then picked up a pencil and a scrap of paper and drew an elaborate shape. "You mean this? It's a spiral that folds back on itself."

All the children sucked in their breath, and a flare of excitement grew inside them. There it was. The same symbol that had appeared on the lawn that morning.

"That's it," said Adam. "What does it do?"

"Ah...what you call a spiral labyrinth, archeologists know as the Classic Cretan Maze! It unlocks secrets, hides things, baffles people, allows people to meditate while walking it, and the making of it can be considered an ancient spell," said Mr. Smythe. "It's one of the oldest magical symbols in the world. It's been found carved on rocks, drawn in ancient manuscripts; it's even sculpted around the side of Glastonbury Tor." He walked over to his bookshelf, pulled out a book and riffled through until he found a photograph.

Adam sucked his breath. That was it! The photo showed the tower-topped hill of his dreams, complete with the elaborate path circling its sides.

The others pored over the photo with interest.

Holly ran her finger across part of the labyrinth. "This is amazing. Who made it and why?"

Mr. Smythe shook his head. "No one knows, though we assume it has some sort of ceremonial significance. We don't even know how old it is, though we are guessing at several thousand years. There is no easy way of dating a path, and this wasn't recognized as the classic labyrinth until thirty years ago when an archeologist called Geoffrey Ashe realized that the terraces around the hill were linked in a pattern and walked it. Here, let me teach you how to draw it."

Mr. Smythe pointed toward a heap of scrap paper in the middle of the table and passed around pencils stored in a plastic skull with red glass eyes.

"Start with a cross and four dots making a square like this..."

"Place your pencil on the top of the cross, curve down and around the top right-hand dot, move back up over the top of the cross to drop down and touch the top left-hand dot."

"Place your pencil on the end of the right-hand arm of the cross. Curve up past the right-hand lines, over the top, drop down under the top left-hand dot, come up between the lines and the top of the cross and then curve down to touch the right-hand dot."

"Place your pencil on the end of the left-hand arm of the cross. Arc up over the top and drop down to just below the right-hand arm, turn in beneath the right-hand arm to curve down and around the bottom right dot. Making a wider path, sweep up, all around the outside, over the top and down to the bottom left dot."

"Finally, place your pencil at the base of the cross. Arc up around the outside to the right and over the top. Drop down left and inward and pass up between the bottom left dot and the base of the cross, loop up around to the left, between the wide lines. Sweep up and over to finish at the bottom right dot."

Mr. Smythe finished and sat back happily as though he had just explained the easiest thing in the world.

Crumpled sheet after crumpled sheet of paper hit the floor as each child attempted to draw the spiral pattern.

Chantel sighed and gave up. "This is too hard."

Owen followed suit, throwing down the pencil in frustration.

Holly persevered a little longer, then rubbed her eyes and shook her head. "It's weird, it makes me dizzy," she grumbled and quit.

Only Adam, his tongue poking from the corner of his mouth, persisted.

"Got it!" Adam triumphantly completed the labyrinth and waved it in the air.

Two blasts of mindspeak hit him at the same time.

First Vivienne's voice: *You can conquer the Labyrinth. COME!*

Overlaying it, Myrddin roared: *ADAM, time is running out. You must all come to the Tor.*

Adam clapped his hands over his ears.

"What is it?" said Owen.

"Is something wrong?" asked Holly, noticing his white face.

Chantel touched his arm gently. "Is it mindspeak?" she whispered.

Adam nodded and removed his hands from his head. His eyes still mirrored distress. "I was blasted by mindspeak...way too loud...it hurt." He turned to his cousins. "It was Myrddin and the Vivienne woman, both at the same time. We're being called. We have to get to Glastonbury fast." He looked across at Mr. Smythe. "Please, Sir, can you help make it happen? Like now? As soon as possible?"

The room was charged with tension as the children held their breath. Mr. Smythe had helped them before. He knew about mindspeak and the Wise Ones. And he'd believed their stories. Would he help them again?

Mr. Smythe gazed at the ceiling, tapping a finger thoughtfully. Giving a whoop, he leaped from his chair, riffled though a pile of papers on the dresser and pulled out a slim leaflet. Opening it he ran his finger down a list of dates. "How about tomorrow?"

"Perfect!" said Adam with relief.

"We can't go until after my cast is off," warned Chantel. "Besides, what will we tell Aunt Lynne and Uncle Ron?"

Mr. Smythe waved the leaflet. "The truth. This weekend is the Glastonbury Arts Festival. There are concerts, art displays, dancing, children's shows, street theater and parades. Terrific fun! I'll invite you to come with me!" He pushed papers around the table. "Where's the phone? I have a friend in Glastonbury, Mervin Green. He's a fellow historian. He rattles around in a large Victorian house on Wearyall Hill and might be glad of some company. Where's the blasted phone?"

CHAPTER FOUR

THE REMAINING LEGENDS

Despite being mid-summer, storms raged over southern England. The area around Glastonbury was hardest hit. Rain poured, thunder rolled and lightning danced. The silhouette of the Tor flashed in and out against the sky as the elements warred.

In the valley people scurried around, tightening guy ropes holding tents and marquees in place and swathing plastic sheets over the speakers on the outdoor stage set up for next day's opening of the Glastonbury Arts Festival.

Many looked nervously at the sky and crossed their fingers, wishing for clear skies during the weekend. Others looked at the sodden fields and wondered how much water the drainage ditches could hold.

Inside the Portal, their voices concealed by the sound of the storm, Vivienne and Zorianna clashed.

"How dare you mislead me, Portal Keeper," shouted the emissary. "Twice you have wasted my time. I will not allow you to do so a third time. This is not a game. If I wished to visit other worlds in this galaxy I have the power to do so without your tricks. How dare you. I demanded entry to Gaia."

Vivienne refused. "You may not pass. I read your heart. You wish to bring destruction to Gaia."

"LISTEN CAREFULLY, PORTAL KEEPER," the emissary roared. Her voice rolled and echoed around the black tower, cloaked in the rumblings of thunder.

"I hear you," said Vivienne from the inner darkness. "I hear you whether you shout or not."

"And I hear *you,* Portal Keeper," hissed the voice. "I too read heart-thoughts, for I am Zorianna, deputy for the Dark Being. My skills equal yours, and I read desire! Your desire for freedom has seeped into the very rocks of this place. Give me entrance, and I will offer you escape."

"*You* are willing to take my place?"

Zorianna smiled contemptuously. "I think not. But let me enter Gaia, and I will bring you a human child who will."

Vivienne smirked. Zorianna did not know she had

already reached a child's mind, but it would be good to have a second child in reserve.

"I have been watching Gaia," continued Zorianna. "I am learning about its inhabitants. They crave power. A human child will not be able to resist your offer once it tastes Old Magic." She chuckled again. "Give me the freedom to roam Gaia, and soon you will be released."

Vivienne considered. "I too sense desire. Yours, Zorianna! Your heart is filled with a desire for power. You will destroy anything in your path. As Portal Keeper, I am forbidden to allow entry to those who will destroy Gaia. You may not enter."

"Look deeper, Portal Keeper. I have reconsidered. I will help the Dark Being destroy the Wise Ones, but I will save Gaia. I wish this place for myself. The Dark Being rewards her followers, and this intriguing corner of the galaxy shall be mine. I have been observing Gaia. Once the treasure I seek is found, exploiting the humans offers much more fun than destruction. That is allowed, is it not?"

Vivienne considered for a moment. "It is not disallowed," she said. If the threat of Gaia's destruction was removed, entry was at her discretion, but could she trust the emissary?

Vivienne probed Zorianna's mind again.

Zorianna's mind was deep and devious. It held a tremendous lust for power. It held jealousy. Vivienne mind-probed deeper and deeper and finally gave a little sigh of satisfaction. She'd found Zorianna's secret weakness: Hidden deep in Zorianna's heart was jealousy of her leader, the Dark Being. Zorianna would not destroy Gaia; she would use it as her base. Zorianna believed she could learn about Old Magic and Earth Magic from the humans and discover the means to destroy the Wise Ones herself. She dreamed of standing beside the Dark Being as an equal.

Vivienne smiled. Zorianna did not understand Gaia's humans, but that was for her to discover. Besides, two could play at exploitation. Zorianna was powerful. She could be of use.

"Earn my trust, Zorianna. I will allow the magic of your mind to probe through the Portal to complete a task."

"I am listening," Zorianna murmured.

"You say you can reach a human child. Prove it. Draw a child into the Portal without harming either the child or Gaia. Then I will give you entrance."

The children's afternoon was full of activity as Lynne and Ron helped them pack for the unexpected weekend trip.

Holly organized herself quickly. She packed everything she could, loaded dirty clothes into the washing machine and wandered out to the garden.

At last the rain had stopped, and the sun was peeking through gaps in the clouds. Holly checked around. Everyone was busy. Good. All afternoon she'd fought a powerful urge to walk the labyrinth. She knew it was destroyed. She herself had raked it from the lawn that morning, but somehow the labyrinth was calling her. Had it reappeared?

The sun shone weakly through the clouds, and the grass sparkled with a million droplets of rain, but to Holly's amazement only part of the lawn was wet. The place where the labyrinth had swirled was dry; the lawn held a ghost image of the loops, outlined by shimmering grass. The urge was more than she could resist. Besides, she was tired of waiting for the Lady. She wanted a part in this new adventure. Holly stepped inside the labyrinth's pattern and began to walk along the curves.

The curves looped back and forth hypnotically, and as she neared the center Holly felt strangely dizzy! She had experienced the same feeling at Mr. Smythe's when she had tried to draw the labyrinth. She rubbed her head and carried on. With each step the weird feeling grew stronger.

There...she'd done it! She had reached the labyrinth's heart.

Come, said a voice in her head.

Holly jumped. It was mindspeak. She gathered her courage. "Who's there?"

Come and see, murmured the voice.

The labyrinth whirled and sucked her inside.

***

Darkness surrounded Holly. She was floating in nothing—no sound, no feeling, just blackness. She closed her eyes, wishing for a floor and, with a small bump, found herself sitting on a smooth hard surface.

Her eyes strained in an effort to find a glimmer of light, but the darkness was complete. She lifted her arms and swung them from side to side. They touched nothing. She sensed a great space around her. "Maybe I'm in a cave," she thought.

Immediately she became aware of cavernous walls and heard the distant sound of dripping water. She shifted her feet and stretched her legs. The tiny rustles made by the movement of her clothes and heels on the rock floor echoed.

Strangely, she wasn't scared. I wish there was a bit of light, she thought. The darkness lifted, as though the remains of daylight had sneaked into the cavern.

Holly peered into the deep shadows. Something or someone was reacting to her thoughts, making things happen. "Hello," she called out, her voice wavering.

"You are not the one," a voice answered.

The voice enveloped her, surrounded her. She couldn't tell if it was a real voice, or inside her head. It just was!

"Not which one?" asked Holly.

"The Magic Child whose dreams I entered."

"I am a Magic Child," said Holly crossly. "Who are you, and where am I?"

"A second Magic Child…How interesting…Has Zorianna succeeded already?" said the voice, as though talking to itself.

"Has who succeeded?" said Holly. "I don't know what you're talking about."

There was a pause, and the voice spoke again. "Where would you like to be?"

"What?" Holly was flustered.

"You asked where you were, so I am asking where you would like to be?"

"I've no idea. Who are you anyway?"

"Who would you like me to be?"

Holly didn't answer right away. This was irritating magic. She must be careful. She tried another approach. "Why am I here?"

"Why would you like to be here?"

Holly rephrased her next sentence. "I walked the Spiral Labyrinth."

"Ah," said the voice. "A second Magic Child from the same place as the first. How interesting. You saw my sign and walked it? Walking the labyrinth opens up human minds. Yours drew you into the Portal. The Portal has many doors. Which would you like to enter?"

"None right now, thank you," replied Holly firmly.

"This was a mistake. Can you send me back home, please?"

"You have entered the Portal; you must go through a door. Choose. What is in your heart and mind?"

Holly's mind whirred. What was in her heart and mind? Home was, but before she could speak she heard the voice again.

"Yes, you could go home, child, but other thoughts are stronger. The portal reacts to thoughts deep in your heart."

Holly examined her thoughts carefully. The voice was right. Her sensible reaction was to go home, but something else told her this was Old Magic, and she should take advantage of it. She really wasn't thinking about home; she was thinking about Glastonbury. They were being called to Glastonbury Tor and its Labyrinth. Why?

The moment she asked herself that question, a shaft of light cleft the dimness of the Portal, illuminating the cavern and revealing an archway in the rock wall opposite.

Holly scrambled to her feet.

A curtain of mist hung within the archway. A puff of wind stirred the mist. Fresh air rippled around Holly. On the breath of the breeze came smells of water, wet mud and wood smoke, faint sounds of splashing, quacking and an unfamiliar rustling.

Holly crossed the cavern, clutched the edge of the magical archway with one hand and leaned through the mist to peer beyond.

She was in the middle of a reed bed.

Spear-like leaves and stems, taller than herself, taller than an adult, swayed and rustled around her. Holly stepped forward and parted the nearest reeds.

A peaceful landscape of marshes and water stretched to a horizon. She was on the edge of a vast shallow lake scattered with small reedy islands. Only one island that she could see was of any size. It rose as a hill from the middle of the lake and dominated the view. Its shape was unmistakable—Glastonbury Tor without its tower. Holly could see the spiral path up the side. The portal was showing her Glastonbury Tor in the past. Why?

A family of foraging ducks caught her attention, dabbling and splashing on the edge of the nearest patch of reeds. A faint haze of blue smoke drifted from the center of the reeds and hung above them. A passing breeze made the smoke dance and the reeds sway. Beyond the reeds, Holly caught tantalizing glimpses of what looked like the thatched roofs of large circular huts.

A sucking sound made Holly look down. She was standing on a narrow soggy pathway. Not an animal trail but a track built from short logs pressed into the mud and covered by mats of thin woven branches. The path offered firm footing over the waterlogged ground.

A whistle cut through the air.

The ground shivered. Someone or something was using the track.

Holly shrank back through the reeds, but the arch-way behind her was gone.

Three young men dressed in skin tunics and carrying wooden spears ran softly along the track, brushing past her as though she was invisible.

Maybe she was! She hoped so, for there was no return.

Gathering all her courage, Holly stepped onto the still-vibrating path and followed the men.

⁂

"It begins!" shouted Vivienne as Holly disappeared through the archway. "After lifetimes of effort I finally ensnare the minds of not one but two Magic Children. Watch out Old Magic, for now I have the means to break the bonds that bind me. Once a child is offered the power I wield, it will wish to use it!"

She swung her sword, and light flashed from its blade, glinting off her ringed fingers. "So...how best to make them do my bidding? The boy is headstrong but weakened by worry. The girl is strong and clever but overly careful and conscientious. Which to approach and how? The boy was threatened by me as the warrior, but the girl was intrigued when I remained cloaked in dark-ness. What shape should I use to inspire both authority and confidence?" As she murmured to herself, Vivienne changed shape from warrior, to simple peasant girl, to modern middle-aged farmwife, to medieval woman wearing a long cloak...

"PORTAL KEEPER, ATTEND ME!"

Vivienne froze as Zorianna's voice rang through the portal. "HEED MY WARNING. DO NOT PLAY GAMES WITH ME LIKE YOU DO WITH THE HUMANS." Zorianna's voice dropped to a hiss. "I have proved my power. I mind-probed and brought you a child as asked."

Vivienne grimaced. In what way could Zorianna lay claim to this second child? It had not come at Zorianna's bidding; it had walked Vivienne's labyrinth. "You think you brought the child here?" she challenged. "It was my labyrinth she walked."

Zorianna snorted. "I made her long to walk it. I learned from the child's mind. She unknowingly revealed information about the Wise Ones and their tools."

Vivienne tensed and cloaked herself in the dark anonymity of the Portal. Zorianna must not learn that she too had knowledge of a Wise One's tool.

Zorianna's voice hardened. "Now keep your part of our bargain, Vivienne. I demand to enter the Portal."

"And if it remains closed?"

"I WILL DESTROY YOU."

Vivienne's voice held a hint of amusement. "You know you cannot destroy either the Portal or its Keeper."

"I cannot, but if I report to the Dark Being, she will shatter both you and your Portal. Reconsider, Vivienne. Would you not rather deal with me?"

"I would. I was testing you. You care not for Gaia, only for the power it might give you. Gaia's destruction is still an option in your heart, Zorianna."

Zorianna stamped her foot. "All right, I will promise. I swear on the stars that I will not destroy Gaia. I wish to find the tool hidden here, to bend Gaia's inhabitants to my will and to learn their powerful Earth Magic. Does that satisfy you, Portal Keeper? It is the truth."

Vivienne smiled in the darkness. Humans were not easily used, nor was their Earth Magic. She thought fleetingly of the Crystal Cave, then re-cloaked her thoughts in blackness. The staff was well hidden. Neither she, nor the Myrddin, knew what Earth Magic had been used to make the magic seal. Zorianna would fail. Vivienne's smile broadened. She would enjoy watching Zorianna deal with the humans. Both were in for a shock! And if Zorianna discovered the importance of the Crystal Cave? Any tampering would bring down the wrath of the Myrddin. That too would be interesting!

Finally Vivienne spoke. "Yes, Zorianna. You may enter Gaia."

CHAPTER FIVE

Stories of Old

The track beneath Holly's feet gave at each step with a little sigh. The sensation was pleasant, almost springy, and much more fun than walking on pavement. At first Holly stepped slowly and carefully, testing each step in case she sank into the marsh beneath, but the track makers knew their job. The woven mat of branches, though it dipped at each footfall and sometimes water oozed between the cracks, diffused her weight, so she could walk through the marsh with confidence.

The trail seemed long, for the track wound its way through the reeds. At first Holly was glad to hide, but as the trail lengthened, she grew anxious and kept parting and peering between reeds on either side, trying to see her destination while remaining hidden.

The day was hot, insects buzzed and bit, and sweat beaded Holly's face and trickled down the back of her neck. Pausing to wipe her face, she heard faint voices. Slowly she crept forward. The ground grew firmer. The track had brought her to a low mud bank, and the reeds gave way to an alder thicket and brambles. She peered through the branches.

Three round wooden huts stood in a clearing. Holly crept into the thicket to observe.

"Arto...leave well alone." It was a girl's voice, high with tension. "Utha will kill you."

A young man, dressed in skins like the others Holly had seen, stepped from the open doorway of the middle hut. He wore a roughly woven blanket across one shoulder and a bow and quiver full of arrows across his back. In addition he carried a spear in one hand and a dagger in his belt. In his other hand he cradled a small bronze bowl.

A young woman, a baby bound on her back, erupted from the hut and grasped his arm. "No, Arto...the Lady's cup is not worth it. Avalon is no more, so why risk Utha's wrath."

Arto brushed her gently aside. "I must. The cup was the Lady's sacred sacrifice. Utha should have left it in the lake."

The woman threw up her hands in a gesture of despair.

Arto rested his hands on her shoulders. "You know Utha did wrong, Gwyn. You are still a believer though the Lady left us. You partook in the ceremonies. We all sipped the white and red waters from this precious bowl." Arto held the cup in the air to display its fine workmanship and beaded pattern. "We all watched as the Lady cast the cup into the lake. Utha found it by accident and should have left it in its resting place. It belongs to no one but the Lady."

"And was sacrificed by her to symbolize the final sealing of the Crystal Cave and the casting away of its magic," came a quavering voice. An old woman, bowed of leg, scarred of face and swathed in woolen blankets, hobbled from the nearest hut.

The girl and Arto bowed in deference.

"Arto is right," continued the crone. "The cup must be returned. Memory of Avalon must not be desecrated."

The young woman jutted her chin. "Then cast the cup back into the lake, Arto. Go not to Avalon."

"I must. The Lady calls in my dreams," said Arto. "She bids me take the cup to the Crystal Cave. I do not understand why she needs me there, but I must obey."

The young woman spread her hands. "The earthly way into the cave is sealed. There remains only one way—through the Portal. That is a way full of dangerous magic. Do not go, Arto. You might never return."

"Earth Magic will protect Arto. He is a faithful follower of the Lady. The Portal will not hurt him," insisted the old woman.

"But I will," roared a voice. A bronze dagger skimmed through the air and buried itself in the wattle wall of the hut, a hair's breadth from Arto's ear. "How dare you steal from a clansman."

A skin-clad warrior, his face patterned with blue woad, leaped from the reeds on the far side of the encampment. He brandished a second dagger.

The young woman screamed and rushed inside the hut.

"I do not steal. I am returning the sacred cup you stole from its resting place in the lake." Arto spun on his heels to face Utha, but stumbled on a root rearing through the mud.

He fell to his knees, and the bronze cup was jolted from his grasp. It sailed through the air and into Holly's thicket. Without thought, Holly put out her hands and caught it.

Utha gave a cry of rage and fell upon Arto, who dropped his spear as little use in such close combat. Arto rolled to one side and freed the dagger from his belt.

They fought ferociously, rolling over and over the mud bank, snarling like wild dogs and leaving dark smears of blood in their wake.

Holly watched in horror as the maddened pair rolled closer and closer to her hiding place. Then Utha's enraged face was right before her. His bloodstained knife slashed viciously though the air as he pressed Arto against the bush in which she hid. Arto gave a convulsive jerk and jackknifed to one side, but Utha's thrust continued.

Pain bit into Holly's arm. She sprang back, forcing her body blindly through the thicket, ignoring sharp thorns and the wicked whipping of twigs against her cheeks and limbs. Then there were no more bushes, just the kinder concealment of the reeds. Holly stumbled gratefully among them but too late remembered the marsh. Her feet found no solid ground, and she tumbled dizzily into blackness.

Grass blades tickled the back of her neck, and sunshine warmed her face. Holly opened her eyes and sighed with relief. She was lying in the middle of the lawn. She must have been asleep and dreaming. She sat up. Her clothes were muddy and her arm hurt. She looked down and all relief vanished. She was clutching a small bronze bowl in a hand caked with blood from a throbbing knife slash on her forearm.

A wave of fear washed over Holly. "How the heck am I going to explain this?" she whispered, fighting nausea as she gripped her arm to stop the bleeding.

She struggled to her feet, shut her eyes and swayed dizzily. This wasn't right. She'd had a dream, hadn't she? How come she was so muddy? How could she get hurt in a dream? How was it possible to bring something back?

She opened her eyes and stared down at the bronze bowl. "You shouldn't be here," she whispered. She knew the myths and legends. This was trouble. No one should ever bring back things from the past.

Holly stumbled across the lawn to the farmhouse hoping she could get to the bathroom before anyone noticed her.

She slipped into the house by the back door.

<hr />

Late that evening, the cousins gathered in Holly's bedroom and gazed down at the bronze cup hidden in a drawer, under Holly's socks.

"Crikey," whispered Owen. He stuck out a finger and poked it. "Is it magic? Do we rub it or anything?"

"You mean like rubbing a magic lamp? Don't be daft. This isn't a Walt Disney film," said Holly crossly.

"Hey, keep your voice down," Owen reminded her.

Holly and Owen, Adam and Chantel held their breaths and listened, but no adults called. They relaxed.

"Can I hold it?" asked Adam.

"I suppose so," said Holly uneasily. "Nothing happened when I held it. But how are we going to get it back?"

Adam eased the bronze bowl from its nest.

"It's fantastic," Chantel whispered.

Adam grunted agreement. He turned the bowl and gazed at it. "Just think...it's thousands of years old...it's beautifully made. Look at the beads decorating the rim, and its shape is perfect. It just fits." He cupped the bowl in both hands and mimed lifting it to his lips. It fit into his palms as though it belonged there. "Oh...it's been mended." His finger had discovered a rough spot. He turned the bowl and showed the others. A tiny square of bronze patched a crack in the bottom, so skillfully riveted that it was almost invisible.

"Don't mess with it," said Holly, jerking the cup out of his hands. She thrust it back in the drawer.

"Hey, you don't have to snatch," said Adam. He frowned. That wasn't like Holly.

"It's the Lady's cup, a sacred object from the past. It must go back," Holly's voice was fretful. She shuddered. "But I don't want to get sucked through the labyrinth again." She cradled her throbbing arm, now bound and hidden under a long-sleeved T-shirt. "The Portal was creepy. Besides, who knows what door I'd get next time? I might never return." She looked at the others. "What should we do?"

"Take the bowl to Glastonbury, " said Adam promptly. "Give it to Myrddin."

Holly gave a sigh of relief. "Yes. He can send it back. He's the magician." She shut the drawer with a bang and winced as the muscles in her arm flexed.

"You should go to the doctor," said Owen uneasily. "You've a pretty big gash. And there wasn't much antiseptic cream left in the bathroom cupboard."

Holly shook her head. "And say what? It's obviously a knife wound. It's way too big for a bramble slash, and all heck will break loose if the adults think we were playing around with knives."

"Okay, okay, it's your arm," said Owen, but he and Adam exchanged uneasy glances.

Chantel's visit to the hospital early next morning went without incident. Though her leg looked wasted and thin after being in a cast for six weeks, she was pronounced fit and just had to promise to exercise carefully until the muscles strengthened.

"See...I won't slow you down anymore!" Chantel crowed as she burst through the farmhouse door, limping a little but without her crutches.

Adam sighed. Now his nosy little sister would be into everything again.

"When are we leaving for Glastonbury?" asked Chantel eagerly.

"In an hour," he said shortly.

Lynne used her foot to push open the girls' bedroom door. Her arms were piled high with folded clothes.

Holly looked up. "Brilliant, Mum. I need those." She

tried to take the clothes, and her sore arm gave way. Everything cascaded to the floor.

Lynne surveyed the mess. "What a waste of time."

Holly gave a strained laugh. "Relax, Mum. You know Owen and Adam are just going to shove things in knapsacks any old way." She separated the clothes she recognized as hers and Chantel's and stuck her head into the corridor. "Owen, Adam," she called. "Your stuff's here." She nudged the pile into the middle of the corridor with her foot.

Lynne threw up her hands in despair. "Leave room for rain capes. The weather report's prophesying wet days." She disappeared downstairs shaking her head.

The weather forecast was right. The windshield wipers of Mr. Smythe's Land Rover worked overtime as he drove the children through Glastonbury town center in the early afternoon. High Street gleamed with a wet slick, and the multicolored festival banners dripped soggily from lamp posts, but the bad weather had deterred few from attending. The shops were doing a roaring trade in souvenirs; and the pavements were packed with a sea of umbrellas, rain slickers, people wearing extra large garbage bags and a variety of sodden tie-dyed wraps, swathing heads and shoulders, as they moved between festival venues. Despite the weather the atmosphere was electric.

A group of trumpeters and trombonists played jazz on a street corner, raindrops beading their instruments. A didgeridoo player and drummer sheltered in an archway, producing hypnotic rhythms. A mother and three children danced around the market cross, holding umbrellas high, and people smiled and made room for them.

The four cousins in the Land Rover wound down the rain-streaked windows so they could better see the activities.

"Watch for parking signs," hollered Mr. Smythe. "The streets are narrow, and I'm trying to avoid both traffic and pedestrians."

Adam stuck his head out of the side window. "There's a parking sign coming up on the left...Naw, it says full," he added in disgust as they approached.

They stopped at traffic lights. A police cruiser halted in the lane beside them. Holly hung out of her window and waved. The constable lowered her window.

"Please, do you know where there's parking?" Holly shouted.

The policewoman pointed up a side street. "All spaces in town are full. Try Spears Fields. About a mile that way."

Holly waved her thanks and drew her head back inside the car. "Got that?" she asked Mr. Smythe.

He nodded tersely. "Yup, but if we have to go a mile out of town we might as well go to Mervin's house and walk in from there." He leaned on the horn as two young women with tinsel in their hair and gauze fairy wings pinned to their backs drifted damply across the road just as the lights changed.

"Blessings," they chanted, bestowing a smile in Mr. Smythe's direction.

He ground his teeth and turned into a side street.

Wearyallhill House was shrouded in mist, as was the steep hill itself. The car sputtered slowly up a narrow drive. A gate loomed, blocking their way. Mr. Smythe muttered under his breath and stepped on the brake.

Adam leaped out and pushed the gate open.

"Can you walk up to the house from here?" called Mr. Smythe. "The driveway's so steep I'd rather not stop again."

Adam raised his hand as they drove through. He shut the gate and paused, squinting through the mist and drizzle, trying to see the view.

The rain had stopped, and there was a brightness in the air as though the sun was attempting to break through.

A burly bearded figure muffled in a cloak tramped up the drive through the mist toward him. The figure raised an arm in salutation.

"Greetings, Adam," said a familiar voice as the figure drew level with the gate.

"Myrddin!" exclaimed Adam. He threw open the gate again. "Am I dreaming? You're real?"

"I can be," agreed Myrddin.

"Oh, boy! Am I glad to see you..."

A gesture silenced him. Myrddin turned and faced downhill. He stretched out his arms, then slowly raised them.

The mist raised like a curtain and revealed the view.

Adam gasped.

The Tor appeared on the opposite side of the valley, its tower etched black against a newly washed blue sky. Adam picked out the terraces of the spiral path and once more felt the magic tugging at his feet. He took a stumbling step forward, but the gate and Myrddin's hand on his arm restrained him.

"Not yet," rumbled Myrddin, "not just yet. You must prepare. Come." He turned and trudged up the drive. "Welcome to my house."

"Your house! What do you mean? This is Mr. Green's house. He's a friend of Mr. Smythe's," panted Adam as he ran after Myrddin.

"Mr. Smythe and I have been friends for many years," agreed Myrddin.

Adam stopped dead in his tracks. "You mean...does he know...?"

Myrddin turned to Adam. "Does he know I am the Myrddin? No. He knows me as Mervin Green, a historian knowledgeable in folklore and old beliefs."

"But...but...I thought...aren't you from...?" Adam waved his arm vaguely at the sky.

"Yes, but I am the Wise One with the closest relationship with the humans of Gaia. Over the aeons I have spent several human lifetimes here, before Old Magic waned. Your time is different from ours. A lifetime on Gaia is but a few days in our reality. Come...now that you are here we must begin," said Myrddin as he strode on up the drive.

Holly, Chantel and Owen were clustered on the front steps with Mr. Smythe, admiring the view.

"Ah, Mervin! I guessed you were taking a walk," said Mr. Smythe. He leaped down and shook his friend's hand vigorously.

The children gaped.

Chantel nudged Holly. "He looks like..."

Holly hushed her.

"It *is* him," whispered Owen. "Look at Adam."

Adam ran around the men and joined his cousins and sister. His face was flushed and his eyes sparkled with excitement. "Can you believe it?" he hissed. "Now things are really going to happen. But careful what you say. Mr. Smythe doesn't know!"

The children swiftly unloaded the Land Rover, carrying their backpacks into the house.

Mr. Smythe yawned and stretched. "Sorry, folks. I need forty winks; I'm beat. It was tricky driving in this rain." He furrowed his brow at the children. "I know you need to go to Glastonbury Tor, but could you give me half an hour to snooze?"

"Sure, we'll visit with Mr. Green," said Adam heartily.

"Nap as long as you need," agreed Owen.

Mr. Smythe scratched his head, but another yawn overtook him. "My usual bedroom?" he asked as he started up the stairs.

Myrddin nodded. "Relax, my friend. The young people and I have lots to talk about."

As soon as the bedroom door clicked shut, the children's questions spilled out.

"One at a time, one at a time," rumbled Myrddin. He led the way through the house to a sun-splashed veranda overlooking the valley.

"Come, tell me all while we watch the Tor," he said sweeping the raindrops off the table and chairs with the edge of his cloak.

Holly pulled Adam aside. "My arm's killing me. Could you fetch the cup out of my pack?" she whispered. "I wrapped it in a silk scarf and stuffed it in the middle of my T-shirts."

"Sure." Adam ran back to the house and rummaged inside Holly's pack. The silk bundle was easy to spot. He carried it out to the veranda. "Oh, boy, are we glad to see you, Myrddin. Things are heating up. Take a look at this." He unrolled the scarf and tumbled the bowl onto the table.

Myrddin's eyebrows clamped together. His hands shot out and cradled the bowl. "The Glastonbury Cup! How did this come into your possession?"

"I caught it...in a dream about the past." Holly's voice quavered at Myrddin's stern expression. "At least...I think it was a dream. I...I walked the labyrinth that appeared on our lawn, and it sucked me inside." She told Myrddin of the cavern, visiting the village in the lake and witnessing the fight. But she stopped short of mentioning the slash on her arm.

Myrddin muttered into his beard. "Vivienne and the Labyrinth grow powerful." He glowered at the Tor.

"Thoughts of Glastonbury must have been in your heart, Holly," he said finally. "For the Portal's archway took you into its past."

Holly nodded. "That's right. The voice asked me where I wanted to go, and I thought of home. Then Glastonbury popped into my mind."

"You saw the days when the Glastonbury valley was flooded by a shallow lake spotted with small islands. You visited what modern archeologists call a 'lake village,' a group of huts on one of the islands. At that time the people called the Tor 'Avalon' and knew it as the Lady's sanctuary. Arto, though you saw him as a young man, was once a Magic Child like you. He knew both me and the Lady."

Myrddin sighed and searched each child's face. His own face looked worn and gray. He fingered the bowl uneasily.

"Magic Children, the edges between dreams and reality, past and present, are blurring as Old Magic and Dark Magic are roused. It's happening sooner than I expected." He sighed again. "Unknown and unforeseen dangers loom when dreams and reality mix. You are children and deserve protection, but neither I nor the other Wise Ones can protect you against this new surge of power."

Myrddin brooded. The children shuffled in their seats.

"You must help us no longer," Myrddin finally rumbled. "I thank you and honor you, for you achieved the impossible by recovering the talisman and the circlet. I cannot and will not allow you to do more."

The children's eyes widened. There was a babble of protest.

"But we promised we'd help," said Holly. Her cheeks flamed with two red spots.

Myrddin peered at her from under his eyebrows. "You have helped. All of you helped. You kept your promises. But now the balance of Light and Dark has changed and the task must pass to others." There was a note of finality in his voice.

"Hold on a minute," Adam insisted. "What others? There *is* no one else! It's you and us, Myrddin."

"Adam's right," Owen broke in. "Ava and Equus have

gone to fix the Place Beyond Morning. They told us."
He nudged Chantel for confirmation.

Chantel agreed. "Then they're going to wake the
Lady," she added softly.

Tears poured down Holly's face. "This is all my fault,
isn't it? I shouldn't have entered the Portal and caught
the bowl. Bringing it back was bad, wasn't it? It altered
the balance?"

"No, no, this is not your fault, Holly." Myrddin clumsily patted her shoulder. "Old Magic is fighting for its
life. Earth Magic is part of it. The cup may be here
because Earth Magic called it, and you were available
as the carrier."

"Return it," pleaded Holly. "Please."

Myrddin shook his head. "Only a human can do
Earth Magic. Only a human can find the way of the
cup's return."

Holly hid her face in her hands and sobbed.

Now everyone stared at Holly. They were all upset
and shocked, but Holly rarely cried.

"Hold on," Adam said again. "Myrddin, who's going
to return the cup if you can't, and who's going to get
your staff?"

Myrddin spread his hands. "Sometimes it is best to
let magic find its own way," he said gruffly.

Owen snorted.

"What a crock," said Adam. "You know there's only
us...so...so you're stuck with us. Besides, the magic is

finding its own way. We're Magic Children, and things are happening to us whether you like it or not. You didn't make me dream about the Tor and the Spiral Labyrinth. I did it before you came for me. You didn't put the labyrinth on our lawn. It just appeared. And you didn't make Holly walk it. She just did, and the cup fell into her hands. So, how can we stop being involved?"

Myrddin sighed. "You are right. Magic will continue to seek you out, but you must ignore it."

"No way...How can we...That's just stupid," the children argued, all talking at once.

Myrddin held up his hand for quiet. "Only I can solve this muddle, and I can put it off no longer. The time has come for me to meet again with Vivienne."

Adam pushed back his chair and stood up. He was trembling, but his eyes shone. "Okay, go ahead. You meet with Vivienne without your staff. Let her beat you! Then what's going to happen to Gaia?" He stamped his foot. "You can't stop us from helping. Quitting feels wrong." His voice wobbled. "It *is* wrong...I feel it inside...We *have* to help, don't we?"

He looked down at the others. They nodded vigorously.

Adam's voice strengthened. "You need me, Myrddin. You can't get your staff back. You can't do Earth Magic. And...and, you can't face Vivienne or the emissary from the Dark Being without it."

"It is a conundrum," admitted Myrddin.

"Come on, Myrddin, get real," pleaded Adam. "We've come this far by working together. Why stop now? I'll walk the Labyrinth and grab your staff before Vivienne and the emissary discover you." He pointed to the Glastonbury Cup. "I'll take the cup with me if you think it's here for a purpose. But don't try to stop me, it won't work!"

Owen and Chantel stared at Adam.

"I thought he was terrified of the Labyrinth," whispered Owen.

"He is," whispered Chantel. "He's being brave."

Myrddin rose from the table and enclosed Adam in a bear hug. "Thank you, Magic Child. Your commitment is magnificent. I will consider your offer. We have a few hours grace, for the Tor's Labyrinth should be walked at sunset. Soon I will decide."

Adam slumped back down in his chair.

Myrddin patted his shoulder. "Come, there is something we can do that does not involve danger. You should all become acquainted with the mystical city of Glastonbury as soon as possible. It is steeped in Earth Magic and may offer you unexpected help. We will walk into the town center and check the Glastonbury Cup's usual home."

Holly raised her head; her eyes glittered. "Its usual home?"

"The museum in the center of Glastonbury." Myrddin led the way back into the house, found a pen and paper and scribbled a note.

Holly thrust the cup deep into her jacket pocket. With a bit of luck she would be able to drop it in the museum unseen.

Myrddin placed the note on the bottom stair where Mr. Smythe couldn't miss it.

Gone to show the children the
Lake Village Exhibit. Back soon.

He led the children through the garden to a back gate opening onto the slopes of Wearyall Hill.

CHAPTER SIX

STIRRINGS OF MAGIC

Though the rain had quit, it was muddy trudging over Wearyall Hill.

The children hiked in a rambling line, scrambling up the slippery path and over the grassy hump behind the house, then dropping down the ridge toward Glastonbury's town center. They were silent, all with their own thoughts, but their eyes swiveled between Myrddin, striding ahead in his guise as Mervin Green, and the distant Tor, whose mysterious presence dominated the valley.

"Hey, look at this!" Chantel pointed to a small scraggy tree. Fluttering ribbons attached scraps of paper to its branches. It was the only tree on the hillside, and the thin branches were twisted and gnarled with exposure to the constant wind. Iron railings surrounded it.

Holly slipped her hand through the railings, and remembering the Mother Oak from their last adventure, she gently stroked the trunk. "Hello, magic tree," she said softly. Her hand stilled. She closed her eyes and cocked her head. "It's an ancient Hawthorn," she said.

Chantel stared at her cousin. "You're really into tree stuff, aren't you? Do all trees speak to you?"

Holly withdrew her hand. "Not really...Just the magic trees. 'Oak, Ash, Yew, Beech, Hawthorn, Holly and Ivy, magic trees all,'" she quoted. "The Mother Tree told me about them when I was in Savernake Forest. When I stroke the bark I feel the sap rising, and the tree talks to me...but not in words."

"Well done, Holly," rumbled Myrddin. "This is the ancient Glastonbury Thorn. One of the few symbols of Old Magic still known in your modern world. It flowers not in the summer but at the mid-winter Solstice, around Christmas. Its magic is hard to ignore."

"What's with the ribbons and papers?" Adam fingered a note hanging from the branch nearest to him. "'Shower blessings on Kathy,'" he read aloud. He chose another. "'Angels of Light, stop the fighting in Iraq.'" He wrinkled his forehead. "Weird. Who thinks a tree can stop wars?"

"Believers in Old Magic, often called New Agers, gather around Glastonbury; many of them honor and respect the power of the Blessed Thorn and ask for its help," rumbled Myrddin again. "If we are to continue, you must seek them out, join with them and use their strength."

The children exchanged glances.

"Oh, boy, not hippies again," muttered Adam. He'd been deeply embarrassed by the New Age ceremonies held in the Avebury Stone Circle during the last adventure.

Myrddin swung around to Adam.

"Adam, are you still compelled to seek my staff?" he asked.

Adam nodded, but his breath caught.

"You understand you must tread the Spiral Labyrinth alone. You must enter the Portal, face Vivienne and demand entrance to the Crystal Cave alone. I cannot accompany you."

"I know, I know," said Adam. "Don't rub it in."

Myrddin held up his hand for silence. "Then be willing to accept help from others with different beliefs from yours. Can you do that?"

"I...I guess so," Adam stuttered, surprised by the gentle scolding. "So...so...you are saying I can walk the Labyrinth?"

"Yes, child. I have reconsidered. I will use your help, for there is no choice. I must regain my staff."

Owen, Chantel and Holly gave subdued cheers.

"Okay," said Adam. He chewed his lip and stared at

the Tor. Helping Myrddin felt right, but it didn't stop him from being scared of the Labyrinth and Vivienne.

Myrddin swished his cloak. "While I am human I am powerless, my fires are dampened, but human I'll remain, so I can advise you without detection."

Adam gave a lopsided grin.

"*You* are not powerless," said Myrddin, reading his mind. "As Magic Children you have tools. Be not too proud or stubborn to use them. They will keep you safe."

Owen sniggered. "Yup, I'm the warrior—I'll protect you!"

Adam jabbed him with an elbow.

"You can also use Earth Magic," continued Myrddin, ignoring the by-play. "I believe the Glastonbury Cup has come your way for a purpose." Myrddin leaned forward and whispered something to the Thorn. A branch arched toward him. "Here is more help." Myrddin snapped off a Y-shaped twig and gave it to Adam. "Keep this with you."

Adam took the twig. How could a bit of wood do anything? He needed real magic, not a bending tree! He needed something to zap Vivienne or some kind of shield so he could walk the Labyrinth, grab the staff and get out without any messing. He unzipped his backpack and shoved the twig inside.

Holly frowned. She itched to stretch out her hand and take a twig for herself, but she didn't dare. Not without the tree's permission. She stroked the trunk again, but it only recognized her presence. Her eyes filled with tears. She turned her back to everyone.

Myrddin waved his arm across the landscape. "Adam, learn of the Earth Magic in this place. The Tor is obvious, and now you have the Thorn. I will also show you the Red and White Springs; the mixing of their water makes a powerful potion. Gaia has only one place filled with more magic than this valley and its Tor." He pointed toward the northwest. "Over the sea in Mannanin's Isle, where the Lady sleeps." He pointed toward the town again. "Glastonbury and its Tor was the first place in England where Old Magic was found. The remnants of Old Magic still pulse from the ground, and many people who live here are sensitive to it. You must find them, for they will help you while you seek for my staff."

"How am I going to do that?" Adam burst out. "I can't just walk up to strangers and ask them if they sense Old Magic."

Myrddin laid a hand on Chantel's shoulder. "That's your sister's task."

"It is?" Chantel's eyes grew large.

"Chantel has the gift of song. Song bonds people. It will band believers together to combine and strengthen the power of Old Magic. Her singing will help you, Adam."

Holly and Owen grinned as Adam gave a snort.

Chantel flushed. She'd guessed Adam would react rudely to her singing. She hung her head and wondered how her voice was supposed to band people together.

Myrddin laid a hand on Owen's shoulder.

"Owen, your role as yet is unclear, but we will need your quick wits to deflect the enemy's attention and protect us in difficult situations. I do not yet know how or why, but you will be called upon."

Owen gave a nod.

"As for Holly...," Myrddin paused. "Earth Magic is seeking you. Listen to her voice. Come, time is short."

Abruptly, Myrddin set off down the hill again, toward the sprawling town below.

Their thoughts whirling, the children followed.

After pushing his way through the throngs of festival goers clogging the main streets, Myrddin led the children up a side street, Wellhouse Lane. It was peacefully empty. On one side a high brick wall contained an ancient stone fountain. A carved lion's face spurted water into a brass cup attached to the basin by a long chain. "The Red Spring," said Myrddin. "It rises inside the Tor. Drink for protection."

"From that manky cup?" Holly wrinkled her nose.

Myrddin ignored her, picked up the brimming cup and held it out.

"No," said Holly. "Wait. We have to do it from this." She checked that no one was around and pulled the Glastonbury Cup from her pocket.

Everyone gasped and turned to Myrddin.

"She is listening to Earth Magic," he said. "We will take the risk."

Holly thrust the cup into the water and drank deeply. She passed it to Adam, who sipped and passed the cup Owen. Owen wiped the rim with his sleeve, sipped and passed the cup to Chantel. She did the same and held the cup toward Myrddin.

He bowed, drank and returned the cup to Holly.

She emptied and rinsed it in the stone basin before replacing it in her pocket.

"Come. Now we sip from the White Spring," said Myrddin. He crossed the road.

Opposite, a tiny stone house with the sign *White Spring Café* was built into the cliff. Beside the house, a flagged area containing two small tables and a tree was squeezed between the cliff face and the road. The tree, festooned with ribbons, was watered by a small stream that trickled between the flagstones and the tree's roots.

"There's another magic Thorn," said Chantel as they joined Myrddin.

A young woman in a long swirling skirt and a tie-dyed halter-top came out of the café to greet them.

"May five seekers drink the water from the White Spring?" Myrddin asked.

"Darn it," said the young woman with a grin. "I was hoping you were coming for lunch. No one's explored this way because of the rain."

Adam and Owen looked hopefully at Myrddin, but he shook his head. "We don't have time today, my dears."

"Then drink, and be blessed." The young woman pointed to a tap in the café's wall. "The water we use is piped from the White Spring and is free to all." She returned inside.

Holly produced the cup. Once again everyone drank.

Calling thanks to the young woman, Myrddin led the way back to High Street and into an imposing Elizabethan building known as the Tribunal Hall.

A small, agitated woman pounced upon him.

"Have you heard about our burglary, Mr. Green? The Glastonbury Cup's gone. Isn't it terrible? Such a mystery! No one can understand how it was stolen." The tiny woman with short tightly permed hair danced around Myrddin, dogging his steps up to the second floor, home of the Lake Village exhibit.

"The police were here all day yesterday," the woman twittered. "They're totally baffled. Nothing was damaged. The case wasn't broken. The cup just disappeared. Poof! As though it was magic!"

Adam's eyes brimmed with laughter. Chantel and Owen hid grins. Holly glared at them. The cup felt like a lead weight in her pocket.

"It's baffling, Mrs. Rolston," grunted Myrddin.

He strode through the exhibit room and stared into a central glass case. The children peered around him. In the middle of the case was a white cube with nothing on it but a small label: *Iron Age bronze bowl with beaded rim. Known as the Glastonbury Cup. Approximate date 200 years* BC. *Found during the 1985 Lake Village excavation at Meares.*

Holly leaned her forehead against the cool glass as a wave of nausea swept over her. She felt awful. She was a thief, but it wasn't her fault! The cup came to her on its own. She should give it back, but how could she? No one would believe her.

"Don't lean on the glass, young lady." Mrs. Rolston briskly tapped Holly's forearm.

Pain radiated up Holly's arm. She fainted.

* * *

The doctor's office was small and white and stank of disinfectant.

The children crowded in with Myrddin, refusing to stay in the waiting room. "We want to know what's going on," insisted Owen.

"So do I." The doctor's voice was grim as he tied off the last stitch on Holly's arm. "If you weren't such nice young kids, I'd have said she'd been in a knife fight."

"No...No," everyone protested.

"Holly was messing around and cut her arm on some sharp metal," said Owen, thinking fast. "We're not allowed to be near machinery. She was scared of getting into trouble, so we helped her. We smeared on antiseptic ointment and used the bandages from the first aid box."

Chantel shuddered. "We don't even own knives."

The doctor straightened up. "All right, all right, I believe you. Thousands wouldn't!" He looked down at Holly. "You'll be groggy for a while, so go to bed and rest. I've cleaned the wound and given you an injection of painkillers and antibiotics." He showed Holly some pills. "You must take two of these every four hours until they are finished. Do you understand?"

Holly blinked and nodded. "Come back in twenty-four hours so I can check that the infection's responding to treatment." The doctor finished, then swung around and glared at the other children.

"And don't ever...ever again...think you can doctor yourselves. If that wound had been left for another day..." The doctor stopped short, biting his lip as the children looked back at him, wide-eyed.

He patted Holly's shoulder. "We caught it in time. You'll do." He sighed. "Call a taxi, and take her home, Mr. Green. She'll be feverish until the antibiotics kick in. So, lots of fluids and rest. I'll see her again tomorrow."

The rest of the afternoon disappeared in a blur of explanations to Mr. Smythe and attending to Holly.

Finally Holly was safely tucked into bed at Wearyall-hill House.

"Thanks," she said sleepily and snuggled into the feather pillows.

The others gathered in the dining room for a make-shift tea.

Everyone was subdued, and Adam was in a blind panic. He hadn't realized how much they relied on Holly's calm presence and advice.

"Now what?" he demanded. "I said I'd get your staff, but everything's going wrong before we even start." He waved a half-eaten sandwich at Myrddin. "Holly's sick, too sick to help us. You can't do magic or mindspeak because the Dark Being's sidekick might sense you." He gestured toward the sky. "Equus and Ava have taken off." He pushed the Glastonbury Cup with his finger. "The police think this thing's stolen, and the entire museum's on alert, so we can't put it back." He swung around and glared out the window toward the Tor. "And all this has happened before I even try to walk the Labyrinth and find the heart of the hill." He stuffed the sandwich in his mouth and muttered. "I don't even know where to begin."

"Night is darkest before dawn," murmured Myrddin.

Adam snorted and crumbs flew. "Myrddin," he protested. "That's no help. I don't even know what your staff looks like."

Myrddin's eyes twinkled. "So you don't. 'Tis a straight branch of oak topped by a fine crystal set in gold. It makes me look like one of the New Agers you despise."

Owen and Chantel smothered grins.

Myrddin's face sobered. "Adam, prepare for your task by focusing your mind. Concentrate on one thing: the Crystal Cave where my staff is hidden. Keep the image clearly in your head, and the Labyrinth and Portal will reveal its entrance. Do not be distracted or your thoughts will lead to other doors in the Portal. Focus your mind. Think only of the cave!"

"I'm thinking, I'm thinking," muttered Adam.

"I'll drive to the Tor," offered Mr. Smythe. "Neither the Portal Keeper or the emissary of the Dark Being will sense anything odd about me. I'm just another tourist going to see the sunset." He stopped and pulled a wry face. "Even if I have just discovered that my old friend Mervin Green is the Myrddin, and that magic is real. It's quite a shock, I can tell you."

Myrddin leaned over and clasped his shoulder. "Take heart, friend. 'Twas not concealed for lack of trust."

Mr. Smythe returned the clasp. "I know. But it takes a little getting used to." He stood up. "Ready, Adam?"

Adam pushed back his chair with a clatter. "Okay. Let's get it over with." He looked at Myrddin. "But I still don't know what the heck I'm supposed to do."

"Tread the Labyrinth and listen to your heart. Earth Magic will guide you," rumbled Myrddin.

Adam thrust out his chin. "So, that's it? I'm supposed to find the courage to step into the unknown. But you won't tell me what to do. You won't help me?"

"You know better than that," said Myrddin. "I was not present at the closing of the Crystal Cave, so know not what Earth Magic enchantment was chosen to seal the Portal. Though I know my staff is hidden inside, I know not how it is concealed."

Adam dropped his eyes.

"Help's all around you, Adam, for Earth Magic seeps from the ground in Glastonbury." Myrddin's voice was reassuring. "But you *must* believe before it will reveal itself to you. You have the thorn twig?"

"Yeah, in my backpack. What's it supposed to do?"

Myrddin ignored the question. He handed Adam the Glastonbury Cup from the table. "Take this. Its role is unclear to me, but it came for a purpose."

Adam tucked the cup in his jacket.

"Go forth, Adam, explore the unknown with the courage and confidence of the First Born," encouraged Myrddin. "The ancient symbols of Earth, Air, Fire and Water surround and support you. Walking the Labyrinth celebrates Earth. Above and around you is Air. Carry the cup, the symbol for Water, and in the Tor you will find the source of the Red and White Springs. The eternal flame burns in the Crystal Cave.

"Fear none of these signs.

"You also carry with you the support of family and friends who are believers. You are Adam, the First Born—the first Magic Child in centuries to tread the Tor's ancient Labyrinth. Enter the Labyrinth with a pure heart and let it guide you to the heart of the hill. Believe, and the staff shall be revealed to you."

The dread in Adam's heart lessened and pride took its place. Myrddin was right. He was the First Born, not Chantel. His little sister had led the first adventure, but this was his chance. His parents never believed in him. Well, he would show them, he'd show everyone. He *would* find Myrddin's staff. He would face the Labyrinth and Vivienne and win. He met Myrddin's eyes proudly. "Okay, I'm ready."

Myrddin's smile lit up the room. "May light shine on you, Magic Child, and strengthen your courage. You will have a fine seeking."

Adam remembered how light had given them all the courage to survive the terrifying journey through Ava's sanctuary in their last adventure. He stood up. "Okay, let's go!"

Owen and Chantel thrust back their chairs. "We'll come with you."

Mr. Smythe looked at Myrddin. "Who will stay with Holly?"

"I will. She needs protection, for the edges of reality and magic have already blurred in her dreams. The fever puts her at risk. While dreaming, she may travel to the wrong place and suffer an attack she cannot escape."

Chantel gasped. "You mean Holly's not safe? Even though she's asleep?"

Myrddin sighed. "She is vulnerable. Old Magic is seeking her out of its own accord."

"Then I'll stay...I'll go to sleep beside her...I'll...I'll..." Chantel's voice rose.

Myrddin smiled but shook his head. "Well said, little one, but you must help Adam. 'Tis near sunset and people gather on the Tor. You are 'The Singer' and the seeker's sister. You are linked to Adam. He will hear your voice, and it will give him strength. Helping him is the best way to protect Holly and Gaia."

Chantel gave a little nod.

"What about me?" offered Owen. "Holly's my sister. If Chantel and Adam work as a team, should Holly and I do the same? She shouldn't be on her own."

Myrddin considered. "You have listened to your heart. Yes. The warrior will stand with his sister. I will show you how to enter her dreams."

Myrddin threw his arm over Mr. Smythe's shoulder. "You too have a role to play, my friend. You have an

97

ancient skill. Teach the boy how to stay on the spiral path. Teach him to use the Glastonbury Thorn.

Mr. Smythe's eyes widened. "You mean dowse?"

"Yes," said Myrddin. "Leave now, before sunset. The boy needs to see his feet." He herded the three of them outside and into Mr. Smythe's car.

Owen watched through a window as they drove away. He felt very alone.

CHAPTER SEVEN

STIRRINGS IN DREAMS

Owen and Myrddin tiptoed into the girls' bedroom.

Holly lay asleep in the twin bed nearest the door, her right cheek snuggled into the pillow and her bandaged arm resting on the top of the quilt. Her face was still flushed, but she was breathing evenly.

"She looks better," whispered Owen.

Myrddin nodded and dropped his usually booming voice to a low rumble. "We may be lucky. If her dreams remain peaceful your job is only to watch over her from a distance. Do not approach or interfere unless she calls for assistance."

Owen spread his hands. "But how...? If you use magic to send me into her dreams, won't the Dark Being's follower catch you?"

Myrddin gave a rumbling chuckle. "I don't need magic, only an ancient skill. You're the one who's going to use magic."

Owen's eyes widened.

"You are a Magic Child. It is time you learned to access some of your powers." Myrddin pointed to the second bed. "Relax. I will hypnotize you and guide your thoughts toward Holly. Though you will be in a deep sleep your mind will remain active. A Magic Child has a special skill. You have used it already to mindspeak with me and the other Wise Ones and during your dream journeys with Ava. Now is the time to use it with your sister. You will read Holly's mind and enter her dream."

"You mean mindspeak is telepathy?"

Myrddin grunted and produced a crystal globe from his pocket.

Owen grinned. "Brilliant! I've always wanted to be hypnotized."

"Hush." Myrddin placed a finger on his lips.

Owen guiltily glanced at Holly. She stirred slightly but didn't rouse.

Owen clambered onto the second bed and lay back on the pillow.

With a flick of his wrist, Myrddin sent the crystal ball spinning in the air just above Owen's face. "Concentrate."

"Cool!" Owen said, grinning and staring at the glittering globe as it sent rhythmic flashes around the room.

"This is the ultimate cool..." His voice trailed off and his eyelids closed.

Leaning forward, Myrddin whispered instructions into Owen's ear.

Owen's body relaxed into a deep sleep, and his dreamself floated free and began to search for Holly.

⬛⬛⬛

The sun was a dull orange orb, hanging low in a streaky sky as Mr. Smythe drove Chantel and Adam toward the Tor. The car sped down Wearyall Hill and twisted and turned through a series of backcountry lanes so narrow that the grasses and brambles in the hedgerows brushed both sides. It grew dark and foreboding as trees bent overhead, shutting out the daylight.

Adam shifted on the seat. As each second passed, his worry grew. Magic pulled at his body and mind as the car approached the Tor. He hated Vivienne. It wasn't just her intimidating appearance; it was her voice. It crept into his head and compelled him to do things. What if he couldn't resist? Adam shook his head to clear it, but nothing helped. Besides, it wasn't just Vivienne he dreaded; it was the Labyrinth itself. He could feel its twists and turns around his body, squeezing him, constricting his chest.

"Breathe in," Mr. Smythe joked somewhat tensely as he eased the Land Rover around a tight corner. "Let's hope no one else is using this lane."

"What if they are?" said Chantel.

Mr. Smythe grimaced. "Someone would have to back up." His tone of voice seemed to indicate it wouldn't be him.

Chantel nudged Adam and held up crossed fingers.

Adam barely looked at her but did the same.

"This will do," said Mr. Smythe after squeezing around several more corners. He backed the car into the rutted space before an old five-bar gate and a crooked stile. "I don't get the feeling this gate is used very often."

Chantel checked out the healthy looking clumps of nettles and the length of the grass growing along the gate's base. She grinned.

"Come on then. What are you waiting for?" Mr. Smythe opened his door and pointed toward the stile.

Adam couldn't move. "Why here? We're in the middle of nowhere," he muttered.

Chantel looked from her brother to Mr. Smythe. "Come on, Adam, Mr. Smythe knows what he's doing," she whispered.

With trembling legs, Adam left the car. He fought his way through the nettles, climbed to the top of the stile and pulled away the overhanging branches. He knew what was there before he saw it. He could feel it. Sighing, he lifted his eyes and looked from the shadows into the sunlight beyond. The flanks of the Tor rose steeply from the center of the field. There was no going back now.

"We're right at the base of the Tor," he called to Mr. Smythe. "I couldn't see it because of the hedgerows." He jumped clumsily onto the grass.

Chantel and Mr. Smythe followed.

Adam's dreams came back with a rush as he stared up at the steep hillside. He could sense the Labyrinth coiling back and forth around the Tor like a giant snake, waiting to swallow him whole.

He could even see it. The evening sunlight caught the ridges round the hillside, highlighting the edges of the ancient spiral path. A ray of hope flickered in his heart. The ridges were only partial. In many places they dipped and slipped, or were washed away with miniature landslides. Sometimes they disappeared, leaving only a stretch of smooth steep hillside. It was impossible to figure out.

Relief filled him. If the path was missing, he couldn't walk it. He didn't have to face Vivienne.

"The path's damaged. I can't walk it. No one can." His voice trembled.

"Steady the buffs," Mr. Smythe replied as he negotiated the rough field. "I'll teach you how to find it. Can you see two white stones? The entrance is between them."

"There are white stones everywhere," muttered Adam. He kicked a small one.

"No, waist-high boulders." Mr. Smythe held out his arms to demonstrate. "One above the other, sunk into the side of the hill."

Chantel darted across the field and up the first part of the slope. "Like these?" She disappeared behind a rock and popped out the other side. "There's another one almost the same size, kind of behind it."

Mr. Smythe loped across the slope to join her.

Adam ground his teeth, his fear submerged by a sudden flash of anger. Trust his pesky little sister to spot the entrance first. How dare she? This was supposed to be *his* task. Even though he was scared spitless, it was *his* task.

"Get out of there," he yelled as he ran over. "If that's the entrance, it might be dangerous."

Chantel stood her ground. "You're not the boss of me, Adam Maxwell."

Adam lunged forward, but Mr. Smythe grabbed his arm. "Not this way. Not in anger." He turned to Chantel. "Adam may be right, my dear."

Chantel pulled a face at Adam but stepped obediently from between the stones.

"'Enter the Labyrinth only with a pure heart.' Isn't that what Myrddin said?" Mr. Smythe looked at the two children anxiously. "I don't feel the magic. I'm not even sure I believe all I've heard, but strange things are certainly happening, so we better do as we're told. Agreed?"

Adam and Chantel nodded.

"I will teach you to dowse, Adam, so you can find your way along the spiral path. Dowsing, or divining, is an ancient skill that people still use to find water, but other things can be found too."

"Like old pathways?" said Adam.

"Like old pathways," agreed Mr. Smythe. "Once you've got the hang of it, we'll wait for you at the top of the Tor, by the tower."

"Guess I'll sing from the tower," said Chantel. "That's what Myrddin said I was to do. So you'll hear me on your way up."

Adam rolled his eyes.

"Are you ready, Adam?" said Mr. Smythe. "Do you have the thorn twig?"

Adam fumbled inside his backpack and pulled it out.

"Hold the twig in front of you like this." Mr. Smythe showed how to grasp the short ends of the Y so the stem poked out in front of them.

He handed the twig over and watched as Adam copied him.

"Concentrate and tell the thorn what you're looking for."

Adam laughed nervously. "You're joking, right?"

"No. Tell the thorn you are looking for the Labyrinth, then approach the entrance between the rocks," said Mr. Smythe.

Adam shook his head and handed the thorn back to Mr. Smythe. "You first."

Mr. Smythe held the ends of the Y and aimed the tip in front of himself. His lips moved silently as he walked between the two white stones. Suddenly the twig seemed to quiver and shake. Mr. Smythe's knuckles turned white as he tightened his grip on the ends to control the shaking. He turned his body slowly, following the twist of the twig until it lay calmly in his hands again, pointing straight ahead, vibrating gently.

"See that? The thorn was sensing the direction," called Mr. Smythe. "I've aligned my body with the path, and now I can move forward until the twig twists again to show me the next change of direction."

"What does he think I am, stupid?" Adam whispered to Chantel. "He's making the twig move." But as the words tumbled out, something in his heart twisted and he wished he could unsay them.

Chantel didn't meet his eyes.

"Come on Adam, your turn." Mr. Smythe acted as though he hadn't heard Adam's comment. He stepped away from the Labyrinth and held out the twig.

Adam took it, reluctantly, and lifted his eyes up to the older man.

"I'm sorry, Sir. I didn't mean to be rude. I'm...I'm... just really scared."

Mr. Smythe's face softened, and he smiled at Adam. "Takes a man to admit that, son, and it's understandable. Do you need a minute to pull yourself together?"

"No. I better get on with it." Adam grasped the Y ends of the twig and took a deep breath. "I need to... to...follow the Labyrinth's spiral path," he muttered. He stopped, feeling stupid again.

"Go on...walk forward, between the entrance stones as you speak," said Mr. Smythe.

"Nothing's happening," protested Adam.

Mr. Smythe waved him on.

Adam took a deep breath. "Okay, okay." He stretched out his arms and looked down at the twig again. "Take me to your leader."

Chantel shouted with laughter, and Mr. Smythe chuckled.

Adam gave a twisted grin. "Sorry. I couldn't resist." He shook himself and grasped the twig once more. "Take me through the Labyrinth to the Crystal Cave," he said seriously and stepped between the entrance stones.

Still nothing happened.

Confused, Adam looked toward Mr. Smythe who gestured him on.

Adam concentrated again on the twig and took several steps forward. A tingling began in his palms and shot up his arms. The twig quivered.

Adam stumbled. "Hey," he said as he recovered. "My hands tickle."

Chantel grinned and gave a sigh of relief.

"Good," said Mr. Smythe. "You're sensing the energy from the path. What happens if you swing to one side?"

Adam turned sideways. "The tingling gets less, and the twig stops quivering, but I can feel it trying to pull me back."

"What about turning the other way?"

Adam turned to face uphill. "The same thing, but it's pulling me back in the opposite direction." He faced across the slope again. "The tickling's back," he called out. "Amazing!" He began to walk, following the pull of the thorn twig. The sensation was so intriguing that his fear receded and the world faded away as the thorn drew him forward and his feet followed.

Inside the Tor, Earth Magic stirred again for the first time in over two thousand years. The Crystal Cave flickered with sparks of light. A Magic Child was treading the sacred Spiral Labyrinth, and Vivienne was preoccupied with Zorianna!

Adam lost track of time and space as he climbed the Tor. At first he whispered to the thorn and himself. "Follow the tingling. Step to the side. Over that tussock. Avoid the rabbit hole. Oops, watch out for the land slip. Uh-uh, I've turned too far. I've lost it. Good, the tingling's back."

The thorn guided him slowly around and around the sides of the hill, sometimes doubling back, but always winding upward. Eventually he stopped talking and focused entirely on the intensity of the feeling.

Always he held the image of the Crystal Cave in his mind. As he wound upward, the image became stronger and clearer.

Chantel and Mr. Smythe watched from the field as Adam crisscrossed the slope above them.

"Is he in a trance?" asked Chantel uneasily. "It's like he doesn't know we're here anymore?"

"He doesn't. He's divining, working an ancient meditative art." Mr. Smythe patted Chantel's shoulder. "Don't be scared, that's what's supposed to happen. Come on. We'll drive to the far side of the hill, climb the steps and watch his progress from the summit."

Chantel began to follow but paused at the top of the stile to watch Adam again. She waved, but he didn't respond.

A fragment of an old song her mom would sing at bedtime popped unbidden into Chantel's head. "I'll see you again," she sang softly, "in all the old familiar places." The sweet notes hung in the air.

Adam hesitated, as though the music momentarily penetrated his consciousness, then he continued on, disappearing around the side of the hill.

Chantel jumped off the stile and hurried to the car.

Back at Myrddin's house, Holly drifted into dream-world. She was floating like a feather cradled by curls of mist. She glimpsed water below as the mist shredded and parted. Tiny waves swelled and flattened, and Holly followed their rhythm, up and down, up and down, relaxing into a deep, deep, sleep.

Suddenly her fever rose, and Holly's body grew hot, then cold: a mind-numbing, bone-chilling cold.

The howl of the wind roused her. She shivered. The mist was cold and damp. The waves below frothed around a rocky outcrop and beat across the stony beach of a dark and forbidding island.

The island drew her like a magnet.

Holly didn't want to go. She resisted, flapping her arms to regain height and control. She tried to turn her body and fly back into sleep, but the mist thickened and roped around her, restricting movement.

Hidden in the shadow of the cliff below, a dark figure spun the mist into threads and reeled her in.

Owen's dreamself flew in and out of the mists of sleep until he sensed Holly's presence. He followed her. It was pretty boring. She was aimlessly drifting through clouds and over a body of water. He flapped along behind her, livening up the dream with an occasional dive or roll down to the water and back up again. He saw the island before Holly did and gave a subdued cheer. Maybe now her dream would become more interesting.

"Uh-oh," he murmured as Holly suddenly twisted, turned and kicked, as though fighting against something. He watched as the mist thickened around her, and she was drawn down and tumbled onto the island's shore. He spotted two cloaked figures waiting in the shadows, one reeling Holly in, the second watching. They stepped forward as Holly sprawled on the pebbles.

Owen glided silently through the mist and landed on the hilltop above them. He concealed himself behind a crag.

***

The taller of the cloaked figures smirked. "I told you my powers were strong. Here comes your proof, Vivienne. I entered this child's dreams." Zorianna drew her cloak more closely around her body and shuddered. "Though why the child dreamed of the Tor this far back in time I do not know. What a miserable place it was, always wet."

"This is the time of the Lake Villages, when the Tor was a island sanctuary called Avalon. The child came here when she walked my labyrinth. It is still in her mind," said Vivienne.

"No matter. Watch me take control." Zorianna stretched out her hand and beckoned with a long finger.

Holly's body jerked, and her head and shoulders raised from the beach. She looked toward the two figures, shuddered and dropped back again.

"See! Do I not keep my promise?" hissed Zorianna. "The girl is under my control. There lies your replacement, Vivienne. Feed her with crumbs of power and soon you will taste freedom, and I will have the first of many humans under my command." She beckoned Holly again.

Vivienne said nothing but watched with interest as Holly's body jerked liked a robot and tried to rise.

Holly felt stiff and clumsy. The cold seeped through her skin and chilled her bones. Even her blood ran slow. She pressed her hands into the pebbles, forced her shoulders up and made an effort to bend her stiff knees so she was crawling. She stopped as a wave of nausea made her retch.

Nothing made sense. She remembered returning from the doctor's and falling asleep in the guest bedroom at Myrddin's house. She remembered floating through mist. But where was she now, and why was she feeling so wretched? Why did she feel like a puppet on a string?

Her body jerked again.

She *was* a puppet! Somebody was making her body move!

A wave of hot anger thrust her to her feet. This was a nightmare. Who was jerking her around?

Shivering, Holly turned toward the cliff. Two cloaked figures lurked in the deep shadow. Another wave of anger gave her some strength. "Who do you think you are, pulling me from the dream-mist like a fish on a line?" she demanded. "Where am I? What do you want of me?" She shook sand and gravel out of her curls with hands that trembled, but her eyes glared.

A faint smile hovered on Vivienne's lips. Zorianna had yet to experience cantankerous humans and their concept of free choice. This might prove amusing.

Owen watched from the crags. "Go easy, Holly," he muttered. "I'm not sure who you're dreaming about, but those two women look nasty." He drew back behind the rock and tried to think of a way to help. I wish I could ask Myrddin about them, he thought. Memory of Myrddin's words rang through his head: "Watch over her from a distance. Do not approach or interfere unless she calls for assistance."

Owen peered down again. Holly wasn't asking for help yet; she was just plain mad. He gave a little grin.

Holly didn't get mad very often, but when she did, boy, was she stubborn!

⚏⚏⚏

"The girl resists. How dare she?" said Zorianna.

Vivienne smirked. "Humans are complex beings. It might be better if we make her dream more comfortable. Then she will relax." She stepped forward. "Welcome, child."

Holly swayed, a puzzled look on her face.

"Come," encouraged Vivienne. "Let us show you the wonders of this place, but first you need food and warmth, for your journey was long." She gestured toward a cleft in the cliff behind her.

"Do I know you?" Holly rubbed her forehead. "Your voice...it sounds familiar." She looked up and down the dark shore. "Where am I? Who are you?"

"That is not important right now," snapped Zorianna. "What is important is that you are here. Come!" With a swirl of her cloak Zorianna led the way into the cleft.

Holly stood her ground.

Angrily Zorianna turned and lifted her arm again, but Vivienne stepped between her and Holly. "Persuasion, not persecution," she murmured, then called across to Holly again. "Come child. Eat and rest before you continue."

The smell of roasting chicken stole across the beach.

Holly's mouth watered. She had not eaten for hours.

Vivienne gestured toward the cave entrance, and Holly glimpsed the flicker of fire inside.

An icy wind blew, and waves splashed around Holly's feet. She edged farther up the beach. The wind strengthened, and soon the waves were crashing and hissing around her.

Once more the smell of roasting chicken assailed her nostrils, and the promise of warmth and comfort flickered from the cleft. Holly followed the women inside.

CHAPTER EIGHT

Lost in the Past

Owen groaned as Holly disappeared into the cleft. "Stupid move, Holly. How the heck am I supposed to observe you now?"

He waited for a few moments, peering down from the rocky crag. Neither Holly nor the two cloaked women reappeared. Cussing under his breath, he began to scramble down the treacherous slope. He paused. "Hey, this is a dream, I can fly." He stretched out his arms and half jumped, half flew to the ground and peered into the cleft.

A low murmur of voices floated out, but no footsteps seemed to be coming his way. He slipped inside.

It was dank and miserable in the narrow crack between the rocks, almost as cold as outside. Owen was baffled. What on earth had made Holly follow the women? Suddenly the smell of roast chicken hit his nose, and he understood. Following the smell, he edged along the wall until he came to a large cavern.

❖

The cavern was full of light and heat. Holly sat in a velvet chair and warmed her hands at a roaring fire that curled up a natural chimney in the cavern wall. She watched as the two women divested themselves of their cloaks. The women were beautiful, neither young nor old, but both with an ageless beauty, one fair and one dark. Holly stared and tried to smooth her tangled curls.

Vivienne noticed and laughed.

"You are a windswept waif, aren't you?"

Holly's hand dropped. She shrank back into the chair as though she'd been slapped.

In the middle of the cavern stood a gigantic oak table covered with dishes. A sizzling chicken waited to be carved flanked by a platter of roast potatoes, a dish of peas and a jug of gravy. Farther down the table an apple pie waited. Everything smelt delicious. Holly licked her lips.

❖

Owen peered into the cavern from behind a large rock. He frowned as he watched Holly warm herself at the fire. Something was wrong. The scene he was observing was hazy. The edges of the furniture were fuzzy, shimmering like a mirage. He also noticed a weird tension between the two women. He watched. They exchanged glances and looked at the food over and over, staring intently at Holly when she wasn't looking. They were waiting for something to happen.

Owen tensed. What if something was wrong with the food? What if it was poisoned? But why would these women want to poison Holly? He prepared to warn her with a blast of mindspeak, but stopped himself just in time. If he used mindspeak these magical women might sense it. He mouthed a warning, desperately trying to project it toward his sister. "Watch it, Holly."

Holly was oblivious.

"You may eat," said Vivienne, settling into a chair at the table. She motioned Holly to sit beside her and carved a slice of fragrant chicken. She placed it on Holly's plate.

Zorianna glided to the place set on Holly's other side and offered her the platter of potatoes.

Holly piled her plate. The smells filled her nostrils, and the warmth relaxed her body. She sighed with pleasure and leaned back to enjoy the moment.

"What are you waiting for?" hissed Zorianna. "Eat."

Holly prickled with awareness. Why was it so important to this person that she should eat? A memory stirred at the back of her mind. Something she had heard or read as a young girl about eating with fairies. To eat with them placed you under their power, that was it, and you could never leave their realm.

Holly stared first at Zorianna then at Vivienne. Were they fairies? She didn't think so, but they were magical beings of some sort. Maybe the same thing applied.

A tiny flare of steam from the chicken made her nostrils quiver. The food smelled so good that her stomach rumbled in response. But what if it was wrong to eat it? How could she find out?

Holly picked up the golden knife and fork and cut a corner off the chicken slice.

Zorianna leaned forward. Her eyes followed the fork toward Holly's mouth.

Holly stopped the fork in midair. "Why are you watching me?" she demanded. "Why do you care if I eat or not?"

She replaced the fork on her plate and folded her arms.

Zorianna hissed and opened her mouth to speak, but once again Vivienne forestalled her.

"You look so tired and cold, child. We wish you well. Food will revive you, give you energy for the tasks ahead."

"What tasks?" said Holly.

"You wished for something deep in your heart," said Vivienne. "That is why you are here."

"In *my* dream cave," interjected Zorianna, looking with dislike at Vivienne.

Vivienne ignored her. "You wished you were the chosen one, child. The one on a quest, the one with power." She lifted her arms in delight. "Well...you shall be! I can make it so."

"What do you mean?" hedged Holly.

"Do as I say, and you shall have more power than you have ever dreamed of. The power to make dreams come true, to give people their hearts' desires." Vivienne threw her head back and ran her fingers through her long golden curls. "You'd have the power to be anything you wished, to fulfill your desires." She stared into Holly's eyes. "You would be beautiful. Would you not like to grow up as beautiful as we are?"

"Er...yes, I suppose I would," admitted Holly.

Vivienne and Zorianna exchanged sparkling smiles, and each laid a finger on Holly's shoulder.

Holly looked down in amazement as her bandage vanished, her arm healed and her pj's transformed into a silk dress. She raised a hand and felt her hair settle into soft waves that floated around her face.

In her mind's eye she saw herself drifting into the school dance looking sophisticated and beautiful, like the girl in the upper sixth she most admired. A smile flickered on her lips. She lifted her fork toward her mouth.

A look of glee crossed Zorianna's face.

Holly glimpsed the fleeting expression, and the spell broke. She peered at the food on her fork, then dropped it. "What's wrong with the chicken?" she demanded and stood up, pushing her plate away.

"Insolent child," hissed Zorianna. "Is this how you repay kindness?"

"What kindness?" snapped Holly. "I didn't ask to come here; you made me. You're trying to make me eat too. Well, I'm not going to." Holly flounced away from the table and folded her arms. "You're trying to trick me. Who are you? What do you want?"

"Why would we want anything from you?" sneered Zorianna. "You are nothing but a child."

Holly shoulders slumped, her hair sprang into its normal tangles and she was back in her pj's. She felt six years old.

Zorianna laughed cruelly.

Holly's eyes watered. Then pride took over. She lifted her chin.

Owen watched. Holly was trembling. A red patch glowed on each cheek, and her eyes glittered. She's feverish again and scared, he thought. She's always scared when she folds her arms and juts out her chin. *Oh, Myrddin, what should I do? Is it time to help her?*

In the cavern, Vivienne shouted with frustration. "See what you have done, Zorianna? You may be powerful, but you know nothing of humans. The child will never take part willingly now. Humans have to feel they have free choice, that they can choose their destiny."

Zorianna laughed. "Humans think they can choose? You jest, Vivienne. Make them do your bidding!" She lifted her arm and shot a blue flare toward Holly.

"You wish for choice, child? Here is your choice: Do our bidding, or stay imprisoned within the nightmares of your own mind." She swept out of the dream cave with Vivienne running to catch up.

The blue light pulsed over Holly's head, then surrounded her. Her pj's became rags, her hair hung in greasy clumps, the skin on her arm bloated and puffed, the knife cut oozed and the infection spread to her fingers. Holly looked down at her hand and arm with horror.

The blue light spread outward in ripples. The ripples flowed through the cave, consuming everything in their path, the table, food, the furniture and fire, leaving in their wake an eerie light and a strange scene of horror. Now the cavern walls were full of rotting skeletons sliding from the rocks. Their bony fingers seemed to point at Holly.

Holly stared down at her own rotting hand. A piece of flesh peeled off and dropped to the cave floor, revealing the bone. She swayed and closed her eyes. "No...no. Help," she moaned. Cold sweat beaded her forehead. She trembled and covered her face. A harsh sob was wrenched from her throat.

Owen crouched down and held his breath as Zorianna and Vivienne swept past his hiding place. He waited a few moments then peered again over the top of the rock.

"Crikey," he muttered as he witnessed the cave's transformation. "Poor Holly." He looked around his area. It was an ordinary cave, cold and damp but not a skeleton to be seen. He peeked again at the horrors surrounding Holly. "I get it," he muttered. "It's not real. It's another illusion. It stretches only as far as Holly can see. Enough of these crazy games!"

Owen stepped from his hiding place and walked toward Holly. "Hi ya," he called cheerfully. "I've been looking for you."

Holly peeked through her fingers. "Owen? Is that really you?"

"Yup. Myrddin sent me to sleep, so I could find your dream." Owen looked around, grinning. "It's a pretty gruesome dream, like a bad horror movie. Let's spoof it up." He bent down, picked up a loose leg bone and swung it like a baseball bat. "Come on, sis, play ball? Pitch me that skull beside you. Bet you I can swing and hit like Adam does. Let's see if I can make a...What does he call it?...a home run!"

Holly shuddered and retreated.

Owen laughed. "Don't you get it, Holly? This isn't real." He gestured toward the carnage around them. "You must have a twisted mind."

"What do you mean, it's not real?" Holly held out a shaking hand to show him. "Look."

Owen grasped both her hands tightly. "Holly, you're dreaming. We both are. Your hand looks horrid, but it feels fine to me. It's just a dream, a bad dream, an illusion. Change it!"

Holly stared at him, disbelief in her eyes.

"Come on, Holly. Refuse to believe. Remember Vivienne and the Portal? When you thought of things, they happened? That's what's happening now, so break it up." Owen bent down and picked up the nearest skull. He tossed it in the air and swung the leg bone. *Clunk.* The skull shattered in a thousand fragments that instantly disappeared.

Holly screamed and hid her face in her hands again.

Owen laughed. "Don't be scared. Those women are playing mind games with you. Don't let them."

"How?" Holly's voice was muffled. She didn't dare look up.

Owen squatted beside her. "Your arm made you sick and feverish, and we took you to the doctor's. Remember?" he said gently.

Holly nodded.

"Did you think the gash was so infected that you were dying?"

Holly gulped and nodded again.

Owen stroked her hand gently. "That's the fear they used." As he stroked her arm the swelling and infection disappeared, the bandage reappeared and the hand healed to look normal again. "See, it was a mind game."

Holly smiled through her tears and watched as the illusion faded. There she sat—a normal-looking pj-clad kid again.

"How did you know it wasn't real?" whispered Holly.

"I saw it happen."

Holly's eyes widened.

"Myrddin hypnotized me so I could fall asleep and enter your dream to help you," said Owen gently. "Those cloaked women also entered your dream. They made you long for power and see stuff that wasn't there, like the table full of food."

"The food was real," groaned Holly. "It smelled so good."

"But it vanished, didn't it?"

Holly nodded and sniffed. She wiped her nose on her sleeve.

"So, now they're using your thoughts to show you scary stuff, like dead people. But they're not real either.

You're having a fever dream, a nightmare. Change it." Owen looked around and grinned. "I didn't know you were scared of skeletons."

Holly shuddered. "The doctor said I might have died. This is what happens when you die."

"Don't be daft," said Owen briskly. "You're not dying. You're taking antibiotics and getting better." He looked around at the bones. "This reminds me of something." He laughed. "I know...It's the cellar of the haunted house we visited last Halloween." Owen stood up and gestured. "See, Holly?...It's just another memory they're using. Stuff these skeletons back in the ground where they belong. They're no more real than that table full of food. Force your mind to think of something else." Owen paused. "Or I could go around smashing things to prove it." He brandished the leg bone with relish.

Holly moaned.

"I mean it." Owen swung the bone. *Clunk*. Another skull shattered. *Plink, plink, plink*. Several ribs fell to the ground as Owen dragged his bat along the front of a skeleton. He roared with laughter and watched with interest as the rest of the skeleton dissolved and faded away. "See? Easy come, easy go."

He glanced over at Holly. She sat on the rock with a look of fierce concentration on her face. He joined her.

Bit by bit the carnage around them grew faint and insubstantial until they were sitting in a normal-looking cave.

"Brilliant," Owen said. "Now let's get out of here before those women come back."

Holly stood up, and together they began to retrace their steps through the cave to the shore.

"If this is my dream, maybe I can change the weather," said Holly as they stepped out into a biting wind. She spread her arms and lifted her face. "Sunshine and blue sky," she murmured. "Warm breezes and sparkling water."

The wind dropped to a gentle breeze, and the grayness began to turn gold. Shafts of sunlight broke through the clouds, and the mist shredded. The sky was suddenly brilliant blue, and the sun beat down on their faces.

Owen dropped the bone and took a deep breath of relief. "Terrific, sis. Feeling better?"

Holly gave a little nod. She concentrated some more. The breeze died away, and the waves smoothed to tiny ripples. Sparkles of light danced like diamonds on the water, and the last of the mist curled and swirled away. Blue sky arched above them, and sunlight surrounded them.

"Come on, sis, let's go home," said Owen. "Let's fly back over the water and wake up in Myrddin's house."

Holly shook her head "I can't...I don't know why, but I can't go back yet." She gestured around at the island. "The magic here is pulling at me. I can't stop this dream. I don't understand why. I just can't."

"Then leave the shore. We're too near the cave. We flew here, so let's fly up to the top of the cliff," said Owen.

Holly's eyes sparkled. They spread their arms in unison and rose through the air to the peak of the island.

Laughing, Owen pointed to a grassy hollow protected by several rocks. They landed in the center and lay back on the soft turf to soak up the comforting warmth of the sun. Their eyes closed, and they both slept.

Holly roused first. She sat up, shaded her eyes and looked over the rocks at the view. "It's not the sea," she said in surprise. "It's a lake. Oh, Owen, look. We've slept for ages. It's nearly sunset." She pointed to the sun, low in the sky opposite them.

The view was magnificent. Dancing water stretched to the hills on the far horizon, and now that the mist had cleared they could see their hill, though the biggest, wasn't the only island. There were many islands, low mounds surrounded by dense reed beds. Several contained round huts. All were bathed in golden light.

"It's beautiful," said Owen, but he stirred uneasily. "But after the sunset...what are we going to do? I don't want to be stuck up here in the dark."

"It will be okay," said Holly, her voice suddenly stronger. "This is where I'm supposed to be. I know it. I even know where we are. Do you?"

Owen shook his head.

"We're on Glastonbury Tor, but in the past." Holly pointed toward the nearest island. "One of those islands is the lake village I visited. We are on the Tor when it was the Isle of Avalon. Now, if I can only figure out why?"

"I suppose that woman Vivienne was the Portal Keeper," said Owen.

"Yes, yes! You're right! I knew I recognized her voice." Holly bit her lip and stared out across the water. "So, who was the other woman?"

Owen squirmed. He didn't want to give Holly another shock.

"Do you know?" Holly pressed.

"Not for sure," said Owen, "but I think Zorianna must be the emissary from the Dark Being."

Holly shuddered.

The two children sat in silence, watching the sun sink toward the hills on the far side of the lake.

Owen jabbed an elbow in Holly's ribs and pointed to the nearest island.

A tiny flat-bottomed boat, paddled by a young man in a skin tunic, nosed out from the shelter of the reeds. The paddler thrust powerfully from the prow with an oar, and the boat responded, cutting easily through the water. It headed straight for their beach.

"Hide," said Owen. He and Holly sank down behind the rocks.

The paddler leaped out, dragged the boat up the shingle and disappeared from sight beneath them.

Holly and Owen peered over the rocks.

The young man, unaware of their presence, looked carefully up at the Tor as if checking landmarks to get his bearings.

Owen dodged backward.

"It's okay," whispered Holly. "It's like when I went through the Portal. He can't see or hear us. We're in the dreamworld, and he's in the past."

They peered over the rocks again.

Owen gasped as the man's face seemed to looked straight at them, but the eyes slid away, and he turned to walk around the base of the Tor.

Holly clutched Owen's arm. "It's Arto," she hissed.

"Who?" said Owen, looking blank.

"Arto, the man from my lake village dream. He's the one who got in a fight and dropped the bowl I caught. That must be why I'm here. I have to see what's in the past again. We've got to follow him." Holly climbed out of the hollow and began to slither down the side of the Tor on the seat of her pajama pants.

"Careful," Owen grinned as he followed. "Rip those and you'll regret it." He sang the first few bars of Beethoven's Fifth Symphony.

"Bu-bu-bu *bum*. Bu-bu-bu *bum*."

Despite herself, Holly chuckled.

Arto picked his way around the base of the Tor with Holly and Owen in pursuit.

Holly paused, "Can you hear something?"

Owen listened. "Water. There's a stream somewhere."

They picked up speed, and the sound of the water became louder, almost deafening. They followed Arto over a rocky promontory and jumped down into a cove. Both gasped at the scenery.

The cove was narrow, surrounded by fern-hung cliffs. From clefts high in the rocks tumbled two streams, one from the left, one from the right.

"It's fantastic," said Owen.

Fine spray filled the air, and the sunlight made a million rainbows dance and shimmer.

"The Red and White Springs," murmured Holly. She stared up at the cliffs. "This is what they were like before Glastonbury and Wellhouse Lane were built."

"Fantastic," breathed Owen.

Holly and Owen watched as Arto cupped his hands and bent to drink from the Red Spring and crossed to the opposite cliff and drank from the White Spring.

"Lady of Avalon," Arto shouted. His voice echoed and boomed around the cove. "You called, and I came. I feel your presence. I come to honor you and follow your directions. For though I lost the sacred cup, you still bid me come to your sanctuary. Guide my feet once more along the spiral path. Permit me to enter the Crystal Cave unharmed."

"You were right to follow him, sis," whispered Owen.

Holly nodded. "He's drunk the waters like we did in Wellhouse Lane."

Owen's eyes widened. "Thousands of years between him and the present, and people are still drinking the magic waters. Wow!"

Holly nudged Owen. "We'd better copy everything Arto does."

They drank again from the streams and followed.

Arto left the cove, skirting the cliffs to climb gentler slopes beyond. Passing between two large white boulders, Arto followed an almost invisible snake-like track that looped backward and forward around the island.

"The Lady was listening," said Owen. "Look how the setting sun is showing the edges of the track so we can all see where to go."

Holly blanched. "This is not just a track. We're walking the Spiral Labyrinth," she said.

"Uh-oh." Owen echoed her unease.

They stumbled behind Arto in single file, winding back and forth, ever upward. The world was bathed in a golden light that brightened as the sun sank. Just before the sun slipped out of sight, Arto stopped before a large egg-shaped white stone sunk in the hillside below the peak of the Tor.

The children watched as Arto leaned his weight against the stone and pushed and shoved with all his strength.

"Looks like he's trying to open it," hissed Owen.

The stone was immovable.

Arto knelt before the stone, touched his head to the earth and lifted his face to the sky. His lips moved as though he was whispering a blessing or invoking a spell. He laid his hands again on the stone.

Nothing happened.

"What now?" whispered Owen.

Holly shrugged.

Arto stared at the stone.

CHAPTER NINE

WINNING THE FUTURE

As Arto trod the Labyrinth in the past and Holly and Owen followed him in the dreamworld, Myrddin paced up and down between the sleeping children in his guest bedroom.

"I must keep the faith," he muttered. "Owen will use his wits and intercede at the right time." He patted Owen's leg.

Bending over the other bed, he checked Holly's pulse and felt her forehead. He gave a grunt of approval. The fever had abated. "You are healing, though your dream is long. Keep the light in your heart," he murmured as he smoothed her covers.

Myrddin strode to the window and gazed out at the Tor. He thumped the window ledge with his fist. "Oh, for my staff. Oh, for my magic. What wouldn't I give to see how you are all proceeding!"

In the real world, while Adam dowsed his way through the Labyrinth, Chantel and Mr. Smythe toiled up the steep sod steps cut into the Tor's eastern side to watch Adam's progress from the peak.

The sky flamed red and gold, but the hill loomed between them and the sun. The shade was dark and chilly. They both stumbled several times.

"Wait, Chantel," panted Mr. Smythe. "I need to catch my breath."

Chantel stopped. She cocked her head to one side. "Can you hear something?"

Mr. Smythe listened. "Hmm, a sort of deep rhythmic moan."

"I think it's a didgeridoo," said Chantel. "Someone is on top of the Tor playing music."

"I suspect we'll find quite a lot of people on top of the Tor," murmured Mr. Smythe. "People often gather to watch the sunset."

"Come on! We've got to hurry," urged Chantel. "It's nearly sunset now." She turned, scrambled up the remainder of the steps and disappeared from view over the top.

Mr. Smythe plodded on behind.

Chantel paused as she reached the plateau on the summit. In front of her rose the black tower, silhouetted against the vivid sky. The sun's glow streamed through the archway, in a path of gold that reached to her feet. Beyond the arch, Chantel could see the silhouettes of people staring toward the western sky. They were an odd assortment—ordinary tourists dressed in jeans and jackets like herself, and several other people wearing biblical-looking shifts or monks' robes. Chantel also spotted flowing gypsy skirts and medieval jerkins and tights.

She stared up at the tower again. This was the tower that scared Adam. It loomed dark against the brilliant sky, but she felt no magic or fear oozing from it. It was just a curious old stone building.

Chantel ran along the golden path, through the tower's middle, to join the crowd on the far side.

The didgeridoo player was seated on a colorful Mexican blanket spread over the grass. He was perched on the edge of the plateau with his legs hanging over the slope and the end of his instrument wedged into the ground between his feet. The magnificent view spread before him—the valley, sodden fields crisscrossed with drainage ditches and the town of Glastonbury, looking like a toy village complete with picturesque ruins and tiny cars. In the middle of the valley rose the low hump of Wearyall Hill, and the sun's rays gilded the rooftops of the houses along one side of the ridge.

One of those must be Myrddin's house, and that's the path we walked this afternoon, Chantel thought, pleased that she could identify something.

Far beyond, edging the other side of the valley, marched a distant set of black hills, the tops of which the orange disk of sun was about to touch.

The didgeridoo player's eyes were half closed against the light. Chantel watched as he breathed rhythmically in and out, making a deep continuous drone that pulsed around everyone. Beside him crouched a drummer, slapping and patting bongos, setting up counter-rhythms that flowed between the notes from the didgeridoo. Slightly behind them a woman sitting cross-legged, played the harmonica, improvising sounds that cascaded and wailed, creating a wild tune as free as the wind and strangely beautiful. The woman's and the drummer's eyes were shut. They held their faces up to the sun. All three swayed gently.

Chantel slipped between the sky watchers, past the musicians, right to the edge of the plateau. She lay on her stomach and looked down over the edge of the steep slope, craning to see Adam. Below her some of the ridges of the spiral path were visible. But Adam was not in view.

She bit her lip. What if Adam didn't know what to do? Treading the Spiral Labyrinth seemed so vague. What if he walked the wrong way? What if she failed to help him? Chantel scrambled to her feet and looked doubtfully at the collection of people behind her.

"Welcome, child." An older man with a long white beard and a staff smiled down at her.

Chantel stared up. He was one of the people clothed in white shifts. His was tied at the waist with a rope of gold. Gold also gleamed from the heavy chain around his neck that bound a fiery crystal.

"Er, hi," she answered.

"Welcome," the man repeated. "I am Osprey, a seeker of truth and light. A protector of the Crystal Cave..." He held his crystal up to the sun. "...and Merlin the Sleeper. Have you come to celebrate the setting of the sun and to honor the way of the ancients?"

"I guess so," said Chantel. She smiled shyly, wondering what he'd say if she told him that Merlin wasn't sleeping but living on Wearyall Hill.

Some of the tourists had overheard their conversation and were moving further away, distancing themselves from Osprey and his followers. Chantel spied Mr. Smythe coming through the archway. She waved, and he raised his hand in answer and joined her.

Chantel glanced up at Osprey again. She had a task to complete, and somehow she had to get this man and his followers, and as many other people as possible, to help. She took comfort from the presence of Mr. Smythe, who smiled at her.

"I'm here because I need help from everyone," she said clearly. Several people turned to look at her in surprise.

138

"What did the little girl say?" asked a voice from the back of the group.

The didgeridoo player stopped. So did the other musicians. The silence hung heavy as everyone stared. Chantel felt her face flush with embarrassment, but she knew she had to go on.

"Do you know about the Spiral Labyrinth?"

Osprey and several people nodded.

"My brother is walking it now...and...and...I promised I would sing to help him, to encourage him. He's...he's in a kind of a trance..." Chantel's voice trailed off. She dropped her gaze and fidgeted.

"A believer," shouted Osprey. "We have some young believers on the Tor! One is walking the Spiral Labyrinth."

Excitement buzzed among Osprey's followers, and several people walked to the edge of the plateau and looked over.

"But the maze isn't complete," said a woman's voice. "Sections have been lost. How does he know where to go?"

"I see him," someone called and pointed. "He's just come around the side of the hill."

Chantel and Mr. Smythe rushed to the edge. There was Adam on a ledge below, stepping slowly but confidently with the thorn twig held before him. He was oblivious to the audience peering down.

"He's dowsing! That's how he's finding the hidden path!" said the woman. "How wonderful!"

"Blessed be! Avalon is smiling. Walking the maze will bring a miracle," said the woman with the harmonica. She smiled up at Chantel. "We'll help. What would you like to sing?"

Chantel shrugged. "I don't know many songs. Just ones my mom sang when I was little and couldn't sleep." Her eyes pricked at the memory. Her mom and dad were happy then, and her mom often sang.

Mr. Smythe squeezed her shoulder in support.

"Sing whatever's in your heart," he whispered.

Chantel squared her shoulders and stood on the edge of the plateau, facing the sun. The great red orb was sinking slowly behind the distant black hills. The sky was spectacular.

Below her Adam crossed the slope, his shadow lengthening up the side of the hill. As she watched, he stumbled and turned uncertainly toward a clump of small trees also casting long dark shadows. He moved the thorn from side to side, obviously having trouble locating the next stretch of path.

An old song, one her mother had sung to soothe them after a bad day, popped into Chantel's mind. She began softly.

> "Come by the hills, to the land where fancy
> is free,
> And stand where the peaks reach the sky
> and the rocks reach the sea."

Her voice was sweet and carried in the still air. Everyone fell silent. Chantel continued with more assurance.

> "Where the rivers run clear and the bracken
>   is gold in the sun.
> And the cares of tomorrow must wait 'til this
>   day is done."

On the slope below her, Adam stood taller. He did not look up, but he stepped forward with confidence and entered the shadows.

People behind Chantel began to hum.

Chantel closed her eyes. The sun's last rays gilded her. Her red hair flamed. She was a golden child with a golden voice.

> "Come by the hills, to the land where legend
>   remains.
> Where stories of old stir the heart and may
>   yet come again.
> Where the past has been lost and the future
>   is still to be won.
> And the cares of tomorrow must wait 'til this
>   day is done."

The last note hung in the air, but before it was lost in the breeze, the harmonica caught and repeated the tune. Several new voices joined in, and together every-one repeated the second verse. The watchers moved forward to rim the Tor. All eyes were riveted on the sunset.

By now the group sang in glorious harmony. They held out their arms to the disappearing light.

> "And the cares of tomorrow must wait 'til
> this day is done."

The sun vanished.

The voices stopped. The didgeridoo took over. The drummer joined him, and a great chorus of sound gave a final salute to a glorious sky smudged pink, purple and gold.

For a moment sheer clarity filled the air. For a milli-second time stopped and magic stirred. In that moment reality and the dreamworld fused.

In the past, Arto had a new idea. He stuck out a finger and traced the spiral maze on the surface of the oval white stone in the hillside.

In the dreamworld, Holly gasped, "Of course! That's the key!" She grabbed Owen's hand and traced the maze on his palm.

In the real world, something inspired Chantel to hold up one finger and sketch the spiral maze in the air.

At that precise moment Adam reached the end of the Labyrinth and touched the oval white stone. He traced the spiral maze on its surface.

The Eye of the Labyrinth blinked.

The four children and Arto disappeared.

On the top of the Tor, only Mr. Smythe, Osprey and his followers understood the subtle shift in light and time.

The tourists looked baffled. One by one they drifted away down the sod steps, their memories of any children vague or forgotten.

The others gathered together and waited until the last visitor had left.

"Where did the children go? What happened?" someone murmured.

"Did you not feel Avalon stir?" said Osprey.

"A miracle happened," said the harmonica player. "The children found the entrance to the Crystal Cave. Blessed be!"

"Yes, Blessed be!" shouted Osprey. "We will keep vigil until the children return." He flung his arm around Mr. Smythe's shoulder and invited him to sit on the blanket.

Everyone settled down for a vigil. Some produced blankets, sweaters and wraps from knapsacks and packs. Others handed around soy nuts and trail mix.

"The child said we should sing," continued Osprey. He motioned to the musicians. "Play friends, and raise your voices so the children will hear us. Let them know we keep watch while they travel inside the Tor."

The music resumed.

Stunned, Mr. Smythe sat on the blanket, hugging his knees. What would he do if Adam and Chantel didn't reappear?

"Idiot. What did you do that for?" whispered Owen, disbelief in his voice. "We're in a blasted cave again. We'd just escaped! What if those women come back?"

Holly ignored him. She peered through the gloom.

They heard a stone strike stone and saw a shower of small sparks. Holly gave a sigh of relief. Arto was still ahead of them. "Keep watching," she hissed.

Arto struck his flints repeatedly until the braid of dried reeds he carried caught fire. He sheltered the flame with his hand until it burned strongly, then held his tiny torch high.

The faint light on the end of his reed flickered. "The sacred fire," muttered Arto. "It must be lit before my reeds are consumed." He cast around in the center of the cavern, holding his taper high in the air until he almost stumbled over a dark mass of sticks piled ready for use on the cavern floor.

Arto thrust his reed into the middle. With a spit and a crackle the tinder-dry kindling caught. Tiny blue and yellow flickers danced under skillfully laid boughs, until, with a sudden whoosh, the fire blazed and the cavern filled with light.

Arto fell to his knees before it and held out his arms beseechingly. "O Guardian of the Portal, show mercy on a believer. The passage to the Lady's Crystal Cave is sealed forever. Grant me entrance through your Portal."

Holly and Owen held their breath.

Nothing happened.

* * *

Zorianna and Vivienne were oblivious to the activities in the Portal. They were engaged in a battle of wills.

"How dare you interfere and terrify the child?" Vivienne stormed at Zorianna. "You promised to help, not destroy my chance of freedom."

Zorianna ignored her. She plunged into the darkest reaches of the Tor.

Vivienne followed. "You are in my realm. Answer me!"

Zorianna swung around haughtily. "You think you have power?" She snorted. "You are weak, Vivienne.

Learn from my actions. The human child defied me. I punished her."

Vivienne trembled with frustration. "You do not understand humans."

Zorianna laughed cruelly. "What is there to understand? The child is nothing. Now she will comprehend the power of the Dark."

"You do not comprehend the workings of the human mind. Humans are clever," Vivienne insisted.

Zorianna laughed again. "It is you who do not comprehend." Zorianna waved her arm and conjured a window out of the darkness. "Look into my dream cavern. Watch the human begging for release."

Both peered through the gap into the dream cavern. It was empty!

Vivienne gasped, then laughed.

Zorianna screamed with fury. She flew out of the Tor and raged around in the form of a great wind.

Above Glastonbury, torrential rain fell.

Vivienne sobered and drew a cloak of darkness around her body, wishing she had never set eyes on Zorianna. "She is impossible," she muttered angrily. "I need to think."

The moment of reflection was short-lived. Vivienne became aware of activity in the Portal. She tilted her head and probed the darkness. Several realms were involved. She felt a quiver from the past, a stir in the dreamworld and a definite tremor in the present.

"So, the child in the dreamworld has discovered the Portal. She can wait. So can the past. Even I, Vivienne, cannot deal with more than one realm at a time." Vivienne probed the present, her pulse quickening. "Ah...here is the boy, Adam. He has walked the Labyrinth at last."

Vivienne flew through the darkness to the present.

Adam and Chantel goggled at each other and stared again around the Portal.

"I...I did it," stammered Adam. "I...I walked the Labyrinth, and Earth Magic happened."

"I know," said Chantel softly. "Time kind of stopped, and something weird made me make the Spiral Labyrinth."

Adam nodded. "It's weird all right, but I guess we're inside the Tor. Earth Magic worked for me." His voice grew stronger. "If I could do that, I can do the rest!" He took a deep breath. "Now for the Crystal Cave."

Wind whirled around them as though an invisible door had opened. Abruptly the disturbance stopped.

"Adam and yet another Magic Child!" said an irritated and flustered voice. "I return just in time. How many more Magic Children are there?"

Adam and Chantel were too startled to answer.

"You have entered the Portal and seek entry to the Crystal Cave? Why?" The voice rolled around the gloomy space, filling their heads, but whether it was a real voice or mindspeak neither child could tell.

Adam tensed. "Vivienne?"

"Yes, it is I, Adam," the voice replied. "At last you have answered my call and walked the Spiral Labyrinth. Now you have entered the Portal between worlds. Forget about the Crystal Cave; undreamed of power is within your grasp."

"It is?"

"Don't believe her," whispered Chantel. The voice gave her the shivers. She tugged at Adam's arm. "Don't listen. Remember?"

Adam pulled his arm free. He couldn't deal with both Chantel and Vivienne. He turned his full attention to the voice. "I don't want power, just the entrance to the Crystal Cave, p...please." His voice, firm at first, wavered.

Gentle laughter filled the cave. "Why do I not believe you? All humans crave power, Adam. Few attain it. Forget the Crystal Cave. You will never be able to breach its seal. Why risk failure when you could be one of the lucky ones? Choose your future!"

The cavern brightened to show four arches filled with mist. As the mist dissolved, each arch framed a scene. In the first, Adam scored the final goal in a soccer match and was lifted shoulder-high by cheering crowds. In the second, Adam received a law degree with both his parents smiling and clapping as they looked on. In the third, an older Adam planted a Canadian flag at the top of Mount Everest. And in the fourth, Adam wore an Edmonton Oilers' jersey as he skated around a hockey rink, holding the Stanley Cup above his head.

Adam straightened his back and watched proudly. Yes, he could do one of those things. It would be wonderful to achieve something that would make everyone cheer and make his parents proud.

The cavern rang with the sound of chanting, *"Adam, Adam, Adam, Adam!"*

Chantel was horrified. "Don't watch, Adam. Don't listen. It's like dragonspeak!" She tried to pull him away.

But Adam was riveted by the images.

Desperate, Chantel began to sing.

> "She'll be comin' round the mountain when she comes,
> She'll be comin' round the mountain when she comes,
> She'll be comin' round the mountain, comin' round the mountain,
> She'll be comin' round the mountain when she comes."

Adam ignored her.

Chantel plugged her ears, raised her voice and bellowed. The song echoed and bounced from rock wall to rock wall.

> "She'll be wearin' pink pajamas when she
> comes,
> She'll be wearin' pink pajamas when she
> comes,
> She'll be wearin' pink pajamas, and eating
> bad bananas..."

Adam swung around. "Oh, do shut up, Chantel," he said crossly. "You don't really think I'm stupid enough to fall for any of this, do you?"

With a gasp from Vivienne, the pictures dissolved.

Floating through the sudden silence as though from a great distance above them came the echo of many voices, finishing Chantel's refrain.

> "She'll be eating bad bananas when she
> comes."

Adam's eyes widened.

"The New Age supporters on the Tor!" said Chantel. She and Adam burst out laughing.

"This is madness," said Vivienne's voice. Her anger was obvious now. "You have followers?"

Chantel shrugged. "Not really. People just joined in." She smiled up into the gloom. "Can we go to the Crystal Cave, please?"

Adam grinned at Chantel. "You've a nerve," he whispered.

Chantel shot him a cheeky look.

Vivienne groaned. She should be using her power to keep Zorianna in control. Instead she was faced with rebellious Magic Children—two in the real world and one waiting in the dreamworld.

These children did not follow the rituals of Old Magic. They entered without ceremony or reverence and did unexpected things.

Safely cloaked in darkness, Vivienne stared down at the two laughing children. They had no respect. And magic only knew what the girl in the dream realm was doing.

Vivienne thought fast. She desperately needed a child to become Portal Keeper, but which? Gently, she probed Adam and Chantel's minds and withdrew in horror.

"Myrddin is close," she blurted. "He sent you to seek the Crystal Cave. He will join you there if you succeed."

Chantel and Adam nodded.

Vivienne's thoughts grew frantic. She had miscalculated. There was too much new magic in the air, magic she didn't understand and wasn't sure she could handle. She must rid the Portal of these two. If they unsealed the cave, Myrddin would come. If they failed to breach the seal, Myrddin would rescue them. If Myrddin regained his old powers, she was in trouble.

A sudden smirk crossed her face. She could still win. While these children worked out the Earth Magic, she would entice the child in the dream realm to become her replacement, and escape before Myrddin arrived. She'd scare them first so they couldn't think easily. That would give her more time.

Vivienne erupted into the middle of the cavern in a burst of light.

The air crackled with static as her armor and jeweled sword sparked with energy.

Adam and Chantel shrank back.

"Go forth," Vivienne roared and pointed her sword at the cavern wall. A new archway appeared. "There is the seal to the Crystal cave." The mist within the arch glowed red and orange, then gradually dissipated as the heat of a roaring fire filled the entrance.

Vivienne advanced on Adam and Chantel. "There is the entrance. Face it, or face me." She lowered the visor on her helmet and brandished her sword.

Adam grabbed Chantel's hand. "Come on," he said.

"But the fire," wailed Chantel, pulling back.

"It's okay. Fire's Myrddin's thing." Adam grabbed her hand again. "Come on. It's easy. It's Earth Magic—earth, air, fire and water, remember? The Labyrinth is earth. We drank the waters of the Red and White Springs, and here's the fire."

"What's air?" whispered Chantel.

"Gonna trust me?"

Chantel looked up at the terrifying warrior-woman and nodded.

Adam grabbed her hand, and they fled across the cavern.

"JUMP!" Adam yelled.

The two children leaped through the flames.

Vivienne groaned.

CHAPTER TEN

IS THIS DAY DONE?

On the Tor, storm clouds gathered and darkness fell. Zorianna's wind howled around the hill. Thick clouds swirled and boiled in her wake, and an enormous rumble of thunder shook the ground.

Osprey and his followers grabbed blankets and packs and raced for refuge under the arch that tunneled through the dark tower. Mr. Smythe hustled in behind them.

"Make room for the children's keeper!" bellowed Osprey. People parted, and Mr. Smythe found himself in the center where blankets and sleeping bags were already spread on stone flags.

"We will soon be comfortable," said a motherly woman. She rummaged in her pack and produced candles and tea lights that she lit and perched in niches and cracks high in the stone walls. The halos of light made a warm flickering glow.

Mr. Smythe looked around in amazement. "Do you always carry food and blankets and candles?"

"Of course," replied the woman. "One never knows when Avalon may call."

As the last followers pressed inside, the rain began. It fell in a deluge that sealed off both ends of the archway with a solid curtain of water. There was a buzz of comment.

Osprey held up his hand for attention. "The children searching for the Crystal Cave asked us to sing. Neither wind nor rain must deter us. We are the vigil keepers."

"Osprey, we're sitting over the heart of the hill," said the harmonica player. "Meditation will center us perfectly with the Crystal Cave."

"You are right." Osprey held up his crystal. "Let us be at one with the center of Avalon. Let it guide our songs."

Silence fell within the archway, accompanied only by the hypnotic thrumming of the rain.

Mr. Smythe closed his eyes and leaned wearily against the ancient wall. He was cold and stiff and very, very worried. Where were Chantel and Adam?

Faintly, through cracks between the slabs in the floor, wafted Chantel's voice.

"She'll be coming round the mountain
when she comes..."

Laughter rippled among the vigil keepers. They joined in.

Mr. Smythe wiped his eye and sighed with relief.

Within the Portal in the past, Arto knelt pleadingly in front of the sacred fire.

Vivienne was too busy to answer his call.

Owen and Holly watched anxiously from the dreamworld.

Owen nudged Holly. "Is it my imagination, or is the fire burning brighter?"

They stared at the flames.

Owen was right. The fire roared, and sweat dripped from Arto's face.

Arto gave up on the Portal Keeper. He spread his arms and called for the Lady. "Lady of Avalon, once I was a Magic Child who walked beside Myrddin. We honored your sanctuary, and many times I heard your voice. Now your sanctuary is abandoned, but again you called me.

"I answered. I am here. Give me direction once more, Lady, for the Crystal Cave is sealed and the Portal Keeper hears me not. How do I enter?"

The fire blazed. Flames licked the roof. The cavern blazed with light.

Arto jumped to his feet. "Lady, I hear you." He threw back his head, his face filled with joy. "May the waters protect me," he shouted and leaped through the fire.

"Follow him!" Holly's voice was determined.

"You're kidding? The Lady hasn't spoken to us."

Holly wasted no time arguing. She started to run.

Owen hesitated, then followed her.

Sister and brother sped toward the fire.

"May the waters protect us," they yelled and sprang through the flames.

Vivienne was distraught. Her Portal was out of control.

As Adam and Chantel leaped through the fire, Vivienne had turned to enter the dreamworld. Suddenly the vibrations in the past escalated into an alarming rumble. Magic was boiling over. A Portal door had been activated without her.

Vivienne rushed through the darkness. "Stop!" she screeched as she entered Arto's realm.

It was too late. Arto had disappeared through the flames of the sacred fire.

Vivienne had no time to think. She sensed similar movement in the dreamworld.

"Where did the new boy come from?" she gasped. "How can there be a fourth Magic Child?" Panicking, Vivienne screamed for help. "Zorianna, I need you."

Zorianna and Vivienne burst into the dream realm.

"Catch them," gasped Vivienne. She lunged forward as Holly and Owen left the ground. Her fingertips scraped Owen's heel.

Owen kicked and vanished.

Zorianna made no attempt to reach for a child. A smile of triumph crossed her face as she watched. She could copy this magic. "May the waters protect me," she yelled and followed the children into the fire.

The flames scorched and repulsed her. She tumbled back on the floor at Vivienne's feet.

"Traitor," spat Vivienne. "You were to catch the girl who was to replace me."

Zorianna laughed. "Wrong, Vivienne, I'm here to learn Earth Magic and locate the tool." She turned to leap again into the flames.

Vivienne grabbed her cloak and pulled her back with superhuman strength.

Both lost their footing, fell and lay winded.

Shrieking like a banshee, Zorianna turned on Vivienne. She pounded and fought, but the Portal Keeper was clothed in moonbeam armor. Zorianna's fists slipped off the magical surface.

Vivienne laughed. "You are wasting your time, Zorianna. You should have helped me catch them. They are now beyond our reach in the Lady's Crystal Cave."

Zorianna tried to pry open Vivienne's visor.

"Desist, Zorianna. You can penetrate neither my armor nor the fire. Mixing fire and water is a special form of Earth Magic," Vivienne gasped. "Neither you nor I have that power. The sacred fire will not let you through. Only a Magic Child goes that way."

"They are within reach of the tool I seek. I demand the Portal!" shrieked Zorianna.

"It shows only the door of fire," cackled Vivienne.

A burst of flame crackled the air, and Zorianna smelled her hair frizzle and scorch.

Furiously, Zorianna swung around to the flames. "I too can mix fire and water," she screamed, turning herself into a twisting water spout that tried to douse the inferno.

Vivienne stood, laughing hysterically as the fire blazed still brighter.

"May you drown, Vivienne!" Zorianna screamed, trying to flood the cavern with water.

Instantly, Vivienne became a silver fish that swam through the water with ease. "I too am a shape changer," she called and leaped with the water out of the cavern's entrance, changing in midair into a nighthawk that circled up into the sky.

Zorianna foamed in a raging torrent out of the cliff and turned into an eagle that chased the hawk up into the black clouds.

Both beings began hurling lightning bolts.

In the valley below, the dikes could hold no more. Floodwater crept silently across the fields.

⁂

In the heart of the hill, the Crystal Cave radiated with magic.

Stalagmites rose from the floor; stalactites hung from the roof. Many had joined, forming glistening columns, some white, some orange. Mineral-laden water, dripping down the walls for thousands of years, formed lacy patterns over the walls. Water gathered in diamond sparkles from the tip of each stalactite and added a shimmering glaze to the stalagmites below. Water bubbled and flowed along narrow trenches cut along each side of the cave, one rimmed with twinkling orange crystals, one rimmed with flashing white crystals. Everything glittered and gleamed, reflecting light from the door of fire.

Adam, Chantel, Arto, Holly and Owen hurtled through the flames, one after the other.

"We didn't burn," crowed Adam. He stretched out his arms to catch Chantel as she cannoned toward him.

"Oh, Adam, look at the cave!" breathed Chantel. They stared at the wonders.

Arto landed after them, silent as a cat. He gawked at the children's backs and took cover behind a collection of stalagmites.

Holly sailed through the flames like a long-jumper, skidded and sat down hard on the floor. "Ouch."

"You daft idiot, we could have been incinerated!" yelled Owen, flailing through the air and landing on top of her.

Adam and Chantel swung back in shock.

"Adam, Chantel, you made it!" shrieked Holly, extracting herself from Owen's limbs. She threw her arms around her cousins. Owen pounded their backs. All four gabbled excitedly. Gradually the peace and beauty of the cave reached them. One by one they fell silent, marveling.

"We need to find the staff, and there are a million hiding places," said Adam. "It could take forever. Thank goodness you're here to help."

They began exploring the glistening pillars and probing gentle fingers into cracks and hollows in the delicate crystal patterns lacing the walls.

Arto stepped from his hiding place. "What children are you that search the Lady's sanctuary?" His voice was stern.

"Gosh...Arto...I'd forgotten," said Holly.

Arto paled. "You know my name? What magic is this?"

"We're Magic Children. I saw you in a dream," said Holly.

"We're from the future," added Owen. "She's Holly, I'm Owen, and these are our cousins Adam and Chantel."

Holly turned to the others. "This is Arto. The one whose cup I caught."

Arto leaned forward. "The Lady's cup? *You* have it?" He was bewildered.

Holly nodded. "It's a long story, but I was hiding in the bushes when you tripped..." Her voice trailed off as she realized what was happening. "I don't get it!" She swung around to Adam. "If he's in the past, I'm dreaming and you're really here...how can we see and talk to each other?"

"This is the Lady's Crystal Cave," said Arto simply. "All is possible."

"We're searching for something hidden here, concealed by magic," said Adam. "But I guess you're looking for this?" He fumbled in his pocket and pulled out the bronze cup. He offered it to Arto.

Arto gasped and cradled the cup against his chest.

"We've been trying to give it back for ages," said Adam. He grinned at the others. "That bit was easy."

"Too easy," said Holly. "Why did the cup come to us, if all we have to do is give it back?"

Arto reached for his dagger.

"Hey...it's all right," said Owen. "The cup's yours."

Arto relaxed.

"Maybe Arto knows," said Adam. "What's the cup used for?"

"'Tis the Lady's cup," said Arto. "For mixing and drinking waters from the Red and White Springs..."

"That's all?" said Chantel, disappointment obvious in her voice. "We did that."

"...in order to see divinations in the pool," continued Arto.

The children's eyes sparkled.

"Hey, I bet that's it," breathed Adam. "Arto, can you show us how to see divinations in the pool?"

Arto shrugged. "Though you are strangers to the ways of the Crystal Cave, you are Magic Children. Maybe."

Holly touched his arm. "Will you help us?"

Arto nodded. "You returned the cup. I will help. The cup and I were called here for a reason." His eyes searched each child's face. "We must approach the heart of the hill humbly and with reverence."

"We will," everyone vowed.

Arto led them through the stalagmites, deeper into the cave, to an open space where a crystal-encrusted ceiling arched overhead. The crystals flickered and danced with inner flames, reflecting the light from a small fire with a pile of dry sticks beside it.

"The Wise One's eternal flame," said Arto. He made a gesture inviting the children to step onto the broad expanse of white marble floor before the fire. In the middle of the floor a shallow depression was carved.

"We have a ceremony to perform," said Arto. With both hands he offered the Glastonbury cup to Holly. "You must take the role of the Lady's high priestess."

"I must?" said Holly, flustered.

"You are the oldest female," said Arto. "And the cup came to you of its own accord. You must do the Earth Magic."

"I am honored," Holly said formally. She took the cup in both her hands and bowed.

"This is the Lady's reflection pool. Please be seated while I instruct Holly."

Owen, Adam and Chantel seated themselves around the rim.

Arto took Holly aside and gave her whispered instructions. The others watched anxiously. Holly nodded several times and seemed to repeat things back to Arto.

Finally they both came back to the depression. Arto seated himself with the children. Holly stood at the head of the pool, between it and the eternal flame. She held the cup in both palms and looked expectantly at Arto.

He smiled. "You have the solemnity of the priestess. Please begin."

Holly flushed with pleasure and took a deep breath.

"We come to the Lady's Reflection Pool for guidance," said Holly clearly. "If our question is worthy, may the waters reveal the answer."

Holly moved ceremoniously around the Crystal Cave. She filled the cup seven times from the Red Spring and seven times from the White Spring. Each time she poured the water into the depression.

Gradually the shallow pool filled, but despite the sparking ceiling above, the water lay still and black.

After the last cup was emptied, Holly joined the circle and settled herself at the head of the pool with the eternal fire behind her.

She dipped the cup in the dark water, sipped, then wiped seven drops over each eye with each finger. She passed the cup to Owen.

Owen took the cup and raised his eyebrows in an unspoken question.

Holly nodded.

Owen too dipped, sipped and wiped his eyes with seven drops of water. He passed the cup to Adam.

Adam, Chantel and Arto all completed the actions.

Arto placed the cup on the rim of the pool.

"Who is the person with the question?" asked Holly.

Adam half raised his hand. "I am."

"Look into the water," said Holly. She extended a finger and began to stir. "When the water lies still, ask your question, Adam."

Adam nodded and concentrated on the pool.

Silence fell. Absolute silence. Even the dripping water and songs from the streams faded away.

The water swirled and began to pull light from the Crystal Cave.

Holly withdrew her finger, and the water whirled faster and faster. Gradually the light became concentrated into one beam that fed from the crystal ceiling above into the pool below. The pool grew brighter and brighter and the crystals duller, until all light was gathered and darkness fell around them.

The water settled.

The four children and Arto stared down into a still pool of liquid silver that gleamed up on their faces. All else was black except for the quiver of the everlasting flame behind Holly.

Adam tried to clear his mind and frame his question simply. "Please, can you show me where Myrddin's staff is hidden?" he whispered. He leaned forward and stared into the silver surface.

There was nothing: no reflection of his face, no movement in the depths, only the flicker of the eternal flame. Adam stiffened and looked more closely. This was no reflection; the real flame was hidden behind Holly.

The flame in the pool brightened. Its light revealed a hand and arm that gathered a stick from the pile and fed it to the fire. The image faded. The pool darkened, and light returned to the Crystal Cave.

Holly gave a tiny sigh of relief.

"Thank you, Lady," prompted Arto. He looked expectantly at everyone.

"Thank you, Lady," the children repeated. They looked at each other. Had any of them seen anything or heard the Lady's voice?

Holly picked up the cup and returned it to Arto with a little bow.

"It is over. You did well." Arto leaned over and clasped Holly's hand.

"I saw nothing. The Lady didn't speak to me," said Holly, distressed.

"Me neither," said Owen.

Arto didn't comment.

Chantel looked anxiously across the pool at her brother.

Adam untucked his cramped legs and stood up. He walked over to the eternal flame and stared at it thoughtfully. He stooped, picked up a stick and fed the tiny fire.

Arto ran over. He lifted a hand as though in protest, then stopped and watched intently.

The flame crackled greedily.

Adam added a second stick and a third. The blaze strengthened.

One after another Adam piled seven sticks on the fire. It reddened and glowed fiercely. *Whoosh.* The flames blazed to the ceiling. Within the conflagration an upright staff appeared with a head of gold holding a fiery crystal.

"May the waters protect me!" shouted Adam. He thrust his arm into the fire and pulled out the staff.

Holly, Owen and Chantel clapped in delight.

Arto smiled. "My task is completed. Thank you, Magic Children. May light burn always in your hearts." He turned and bowed to the fire. "Thank you, gracious Lady. May your waters protect me." Holding the bowl high, he stepped into the flames.

At the bedroom window in Wearyallhill House, Myrddin lifted his arm to the sky and gave a roar of delight. "Light and Dark, Dark and Light, Earth Magic lives...Adam has my staff. My magic flows once more." He held his hands over Holly's arm, whispered a healing spell and sprinkled stardust over her bandage. Holding his arms over the sleeping children, he spoke. "Gently, gently, you may return from the dreamworld. We will go together and greet Adam." He sat on Owen's bed and waited for them to stir.

In the Crystal Cave, Holly nudged Owen who was still staring at the eternal flame. "My dream's over."

"I know," said Owen. "Mine too."

They smiled at Chantel and waved at Adam. "See ya," they called together and walked toward the fire. Both faded away as they entered the flames.

"Time to go," said Adam, holding the staff proudly. His eyes wandered around the heart of the Crystal Cave. "Wonderful, isn't it?" he breathed. "We've seen 'Merlin's Crystal Cave.'" He laughed. "It just doesn't belong to Merlin. It's the Lady's." He raised his voice, "Thank you, Lady."

"Thank you, Lady," echoed Chantel. "But I wish you'd talk to Holly."

Adam offered his sister his hand.

"You've grown taller," Chantel said as she tucked her fingers in his.

Together they stepped into the fire.

"We're singing in the rain, just singing in the rain...," warbled the vigil keepers.

Myrddin, his cloak sheltering Holly and Owen, appeared in the archway, startling everyone.

"Blessings, good people," he shouted. "Your vigil is rewarded."

Mr. Smythe gave a shout of relief and pleasure and jumped up to join them.

Myrddin beckoned, turned and walked through the

rain to the edge of the Tor. With his back to the tower he raised his arms.

The rain ceased. The darkness lifted like a curtain to reveal a watery dawn sky reflected in the floodwaters that lapped around the base of the Tor.

Osprey rushed to the rim of the Tor. His followers jostled behind. They gave a collective gasp when they saw the view. "The prophesy!" several voices whispered.

> "When the Tor an island be,
> A child shall wind around the key
> And waken me," chanted Myrddin and Osprey.

Thud! The white stone fell from the Tor's side. Chantel and Adam skipped out, laughing. Adam waved the staff in triumph.

Myrddin ran toward him.

Zap! Lightning struck the tower. Zorianna and Vivienne appeared on the top parapet.

Zorianna dove through the air in a blur.

As Adam passed the staff to Myrddin, Zorianna swooped between them and snatched it from Myrddin's hand. "A Portal door, Vivienne," she shrieked.

"Oh no, you don't," yelled Adam furiously. He grabbed her cloak and hung on.

"Damn you, Vivienne," raged Myrddin as Zorianna and Adam zipped through the tower's arch and disappeared into mist.

"Watch the children, Smythe!" bellowed Myrddin. His hair and beard flamed and colors swirled in his cloak as he threw a veil of forgetfulness across the vigil keepers and sped through the mist behind Adam and Zorianna.

Epilogue

In Wearyallhill House, Chantel, Owen, Holly and Mr. Smythe sat silently at the breakfast table. In the center, a bowl of scrambled eggs congealed and the rack of toast grew limp and cold.

"We need help. We've got to get Adam back before we go home tomorrow," said Chantel. "Why don't we make a circle and call for Equus?" She left the table and held out her hands.

Owen sat up. "Or Ava. That's worked before. Why not?"

"It's mindspeak," said Holly. "I thought we weren't to use it."

Owen gave a harsh laugh. "That was to protect Myrddin. Zorianna knows all about him now. He's on her tail." He left the table to join hands with Chantel.

Holly pushed back her chair. "Okay." She took Chantel's other hand.

They looked at Mr. Smythe.

"You're part of the magic now," said Holly.

"Indeed I am," said Mr. Smythe. He completed the circle.

"Light and Dark," murmured Holly.

"Dark and Light," whispered Chantel.

"Sun by day," said Owen.

"Moon by ni..." Mr. Smythe stopped short as for the first time in his life he heard mindspeak.

We hear you, Magic Children. Keep the light in your hearts. And on the breath of the breeze that wafted in from the veranda the children and Mr. Smythe heard the cry of a hawk and the faint galloping of hooves.

Holly's shoulders drooped, and she bit her lip. She'd hoped to hear the voice of the Lady.

A clatter and bang came from the hallway.

The circle fragmented as everyone rushed to see what had happened.

The Sunday paper lay in the middle of the floor.

Owen gave it a kick. "I thought it was an answer for us."

Holly picked the paper up and passed it to Mr. Smythe.

He opened it as they moved back into the breakfast room.

"Actually, it does have a sort of answer," Mr. Smythe said. His voice sounded odd.

The three Magic Children turned to look at him. He held out the front page.

"MAGICAL RETURN OF GLASTONBURY CUP!" shouted the headline.

"Yes," yelled Owen, punching the air with his fist. "The magic continues!"

I will never forget my first glimpse of Glastonbury Tor. My husband, Dave, and I were driving through the flat green pastures of Somerset, England, and suddenly an unusual hill loomed in the distance. I turned to him. "Dave, what's that tower-topped hill?"

He shook his head, concentrating on negotiating around a tractor.

I stared at the hill, and excitement built. "It must be the Tor at Glastonbury... I've always wanted to go there. It's the Isle of Avalon, the heart of the Merlin legends!" As I spoke visions of Merlin, King Arthur, the Crystal Cave and the grail danced in my head. The Tor's magic pull increased. "Dave...I have to go there. I have to climb the Tor."

He laughed and turned toward it at the next junction. We approached, cross-country, through narrow winding lanes and suddenly there we were in Wellhouse Lane, captured by the magic of Glastonbury.

Glastonbury is fascinating. It's a small modern community surrounding a centuries-old town center and the ruins of Glastonbury Abbey, all overshadowed by the even more ancient Tor.

The abbey, destroyed by the army of King Henry VIII, is the heart of England's Christianity, for tradition says it was founded by Joseph of Arimathea. It is said that Joseph stuck his staff in the ground where the first English church was to be built and that it immediately rooted and became the blessed thorn that flowers at Christmastide. The thorn and its several offshoots around the city really do bloom in midwinter. Several flowering twigs are gathered early each Christmas morning and rushed to Queen Elizabeth II to grace her breakfast table.

But stories of magical staffs becoming trees have roots in religions far older than Christianity, and the legends of the Tor, of Avalon and of the figures we currently call Merlin and Arthur originated several centuries before the birth of Christ. This is the folklore I used as a basis of my fantasy story.

We climbed the Tor that first afternoon, using the path Chantel and Mr. Smythe take in my story. As we approached the tower, I saw the figure of a knight silhouetted in the center of the arch. The hairs rose at the back of my neck. As we drew closer I realized it was a modern-day pilgrim dressed in tight jeans and a tunic top, hands clasped over a walking staff, meditating over the heart of the hill.

We left the pilgrim to her meditations and circled the top plateau, marveling at the view. While Dave explored some of the spiral terraces, I sat in the sunshine, my back against the crumbling walls of the tower, absorbing the myths and the magical atmosphere. Some time later, as we left the Tor, the pilgrim joined us on the path, and we gave her a ride into the center of Glastonbury. She spoke of the current lore of the Tor, of her belief in secret tunnels and caves deep inside the hill, their entrance lost or hidden. She told of the power of the waters of the Red and White Springs and the beauty spot that had been their source, now destroyed by Glastonbury's water-supply building. She also described a local historian's discovery of the spiral labyrinth carved up the Tor's sides.

Since then we have visited Glastonbury several times. The last time we stayed at Wearyallhill House, which I use as Myrddin's house in my story, and walked into the city over Wearyall Hill, past a blessed thorn decked with bright ribbons and fluttering paper appeals. We drank from both the Red and White Springs and visited the Lake Village exhibit on the second floor of the Elizabethan building known as the Tribunal Hall.

There I felt a magical pull again. As I looked at the artifacts excavated from a lake village site, one drew my eyes. It was a bronze bowl, just big enough to cup easily in the palm of one's hands. It was beautifully made, showing finer workmanship that anything else in the exhibit. It was well loved, having been carefully mended with a tiny beaten bronze patch held on with minute rivets, as finely crafted as the original bowl. It was obviously far more than a household object. What if...? What if this small but magnificent bowl was really an important ceremonial object? What if it was the forerunner of the stories of the grail?

Further research took us to the site of the reconstructed Lake Village. The interpretation depicted a lake settlement of around 200 BC where an original of Arthur, assuming he was a real person, may well have grown up. It was a far cry from the current image of Arthur popularized by books, film and television. This image is based on many later figures whose tales have become incorporated into the legend.

We sat in smoky circular huts and learned to scrape hides, spin raw wool and weave willow branches into wattle mats. Such mats were used to cover the timbers forming the ancient tracks through the marsh, used over thousands of years in the days when the Tor rose from a shallow lake.

I learned to draw the spiral labyrinth, an ancient symbol found not only in England, but also carved on rocks in Ireland, France and Greece. But the Tor is the only hill to my knowledge where the labyrinth takes the form of a path up its side.

I wish I had been able to enter the heart of the hill. I found the oval white stone said to be the entrance, sunk into the Tor, just below the tower. It remained immovable, so I did the next best thing. Dave and I visited the caves of nearby Cheddar Gorge and walked through caverns filled with stalagmites and stalactites and marveled at the amazing formations flowing down the walls, created by millions of years of mineral-laden water dripping through the rock above.

The result of this fascinating research is *Heart of the Hill*, the third book in the Summer of Magic Quartet, a four-book fantasy story set among real landscapes in the heart of England.

As I did in Book One, *The White Horse Talisman*, and in Book Two, *Dance of the Stones*, I have woven historical objects, ancient history and some of England's rich folklore into *Heart of the Hill*. But the children, Chantel, Adam, Holly and Owen, all the other characters and the entire adventure are figments of my imagination.

The children's fantastic adventures do not end here. Watch for the final book in the Summer of Magic Quartet when Chantel, Holly and Owen chase after Adam and confront the Dark Being on an island hidden from view behind a cloud of mist known as Mannanin's Cloak.

Book Four, *Behind the Sorcerer's Cloak,* will be published in fall, 2006.

Andrea Spalding
Pender Island, BC
April 2005

ACKNOWLEDGEMENTS

There are always people to thank in the creation of a book. This book was completed under unusual circumstances.

Special recognition is due to Bob Tyrrell and Maggie de Vries whose patience, support and encouragement while waiting for the manuscript made it possible. I also received special support from Deborah Allison and Marion Ehrenberg—I could not have carried on without them. Artist Martin Springett offered friendship and encouragement and provided a wonderful cover design that inspired me during the last chapters, and my agent, Melanie Colbert, lifted my spirits during the difficult days with encouraging phone calls.

I am blessed with understanding friends, Cherie and Kevin, Sharon and Gary, Sheryl, Georgi and Lawrence. They kept the faith even when I was too preoccupied to phone or visit.

As always my husband, Dave, and our three daughters, Jane, Penny and Lucy, gave unstinting love and provided a foundation of approval and encouragement, and even occasional bullying, that helped me continue working on the days I nearly gave up.

Thanks everyone—we did it!

photo: David Spalding

Award-winning author, **Andrea Spalding**, has written many popular books for children, but the first three volumes of the Summer of Magic Quartet are among her most exciting. *The White Horse Talisman* (Book One) was nominated for the Silver Birch, Hackmatack and Manitoba Readers' Choice Awards. *Dance of the Stones* (Book Two) was also a Silver Birch nominee. In *Heart of the Hill*, Andrea raises the adventure to another level altogether in preparation for the final volume of the quartet, *Behind the Sorcerer's Cloak,* to follow next year. Andrea lives with her husband on Pender Island, British Columbia.

Book One
The Summer of Magic Quartet

The White Horse Talisman

The battle between good and evil plays itself out through four children, a mythical horse and an imprisoned dragon.

"It was seven minutes after midnight on the seventh day. Whooooooosh! A flash of light streaked the sky. A shooting star touched a strange carving on the hillside and a magical horse shook itself free of the chalk and rose to its feet. It was seven minutes after midnight on the seventh day of the seventh month. The only person watching was Chantel. No matter. It was enough. The summer of magic could begin."

Chantel, Adam, Holly and Owen must help Equus, the great white horse, find his mate and foal and regain his magical talisman. But as the horse rises, so does the dragon. The age-old battle between good and evil threatens the bond between Chantel and Adam and endangers the quest. This is fantasy at its best, a story that raises hairs on the back of the neck and sends satisfying chills up and down the spine, a story that, while clearly drawn from the rich world of make believe, feels truer than true.

BOOK TWO
THE SUMMER OF MAGIC QUARTET

_____

DANCE OF THE STONES

The four children from *The White Horse Talisman* seek Ava's circlet, buried within the ancient stone circle of Avebury.

> *"The third sunbeam shot its magical light into a valley. There towered a stone circle, great gray stones veiled in morning mist. The golden beam lit the dew-covered grass. The tide of light flooded and washed each sarcenstone. The Stones were ready. As gray became gold, the largest stone spun on its axis, then stood sentinel as before. The dawn magic happened quickly, without witness. That was to change. Four ordinary children were about to be called to The Circle."*

Chantel, Adam, Holly and Owen are eager to begin the next stage of their adventure. "The Stones have stirred," Ava, Hawkwoman and Wise One, tells Owen, "The time is near for the Circle Dance." The stones are the ancient stone circle of Avebury in England. But the Dark Being approaches, and her servant, a wraith, blocks the children's progress. When Ava is hurt, the children are thrown back on their own resources. They must discover the ritual that will release the circlet. Each child has a part to play in finding the circlet and holding back the Dark Being.